Anxiety exploded into full-on panic.

The fear of plunging into the water had forced her to relive that long-ago night of terror. But she'd made it out that night, and it had been seven years with no sign of her husband. And no indication he'd ever made it out of that lake alive.

How could she explain this to Noah? No one could know the truth.

She didn't hear the roaring sound until headlights bore down on her. She screamed and ran, but the vehicle kept coming, as if calling her name.

I'm coming for you, Melinda. I'm coming for you.

Only when the crowd approached did the car turn and roar down the road.

Noah reached her and she fell into his arms. "I heard you scream. What happened?"

Panic morphed into tears and she clung to him. "He tried to run me down."

"Who?"

All she knew was that whoever was after her wasn't giving up. Not until he killed her.

Virginia Vaughan is a born-and-raised Mississippi girl. She is blessed to come from a large Southern family, and her fondest memories include listening to stories recounted around the dinner table. She was a lover of books from a young age, devouring tales of romance, danger and love. She soon started writing them herself. You can connect with Virginia through her website, virginiavaughanonline.com, or through the publisher.

Books by Virginia Vaughan

Love Inspired Suspense

Covert Operatives

Cold Case Cover-Up
Deadly Christmas Duty

Rangers Under Fire

Yuletide Abduction
Reunion Mission
Ranch Refuge
Mistletoe Reunion Threat
Mission Undercover
Mission: Memory Recall

No Safe Haven

DEADLY CHRISTMAS DUTY

VIRGINIA VAUGHAN

HARLEQUIN® LOVE INSPIRED® SUSPENSE

Recycling programs
for this product may
not exist in your area.

LOVE INSPIRED BOOKS

ISBN-13: 978-1-335-49074-2

Deadly Christmas Duty

www.Harlequin.com

Printed in U.S.A.

And he said, Come. And when Peter was come down out of the ship, he walked on the water, to go to Jesus.
—Matthew 14:29

To my mom, who I often go to when I'm stuck on a project. You probably never thought you'd be plotting to kill people with your daughter. Life is crazy, isn't it?

ONE

Prosecutor Melinda Steele dug through her purse to find the keys that unlocked her office door. Her assistant, Dawn, was out to lunch, and the rest of the suite appeared empty on this Saturday afternoon. She found her keys but stopped when she went to slide one into the lock. Her door was cracked open; the latch never engaged.

Uneasiness prickled her neck. Dawn was always good about making sure everything was locked up before she left for lunch. It was possible she'd been distracted and forgotten, but a sinister dread crept through Melinda as it always did whenever something jarred her out of her normal routine.

Stop being so paranoid, she told herself as she tried to shake off those fears of bygone days when she constantly peered over her shoulder, always watching for the bad thing that was coming for her and her son. But Ramey was now six years old, and the big bad man had never come for them. They were safe here in Daytonville, Alabama, safe in the comfort and anonymity of the small-town life she'd grown to love.

She pushed open her door and walked inside, scanning her office. Everything looked fine. Everything was in its place, and nothing looked askew. That helped reassure her that she was being oversensitive. She touched the photo of Ramey on her desk as she walked by it and sat down. He was fine. They were both fine. They'd escaped the past, and no one was coming for them now. And the door had been locked. Dawn had simply forgotten to pull it shut all the way. It was nothing but a mistake.

She turned on her computer and took out a case file she needed to update as it went through the screens of booting up. A knock on the door grabbed her attention, and she looked up into the most beautiful deep green, long-lashed eyes of a man she'd ever seen. The rest of his face was masculine and his jaw strong. His broad shoulders filled the doorway, but he wasn't a large man, just fit.

He stepped inside and extended his hand to shake. "Miss Steele? My name is Noah Cason. I'm Nikki Lassiter's brother. I was hoping I could have a moment to speak with you."

Nikki's brother. The former Navy SEAL. That explained the muscles, as well as the hauntingly familiar eyes she'd seen staring at her from a photo on his sister's mantel.

She stood and gripped his hand. It was strong and intense. "Certainly. Won't you sit down? I knew your sister very well. She was my son's teacher two years ago and we became close friends. I'm very sorry for your loss."

The words seemed empty even to her as she spoke them, but what else could she say? Sorry the man who was supposed to protect your sister was a monster in disguise? Sorry your kid sister has vanished without a trace and is probably dead?

"Thank you." He sat, but she noticed the way he scanned the room, probably memorizing each and every detail. She smiled, recalling how Nikki had told her about his tendency to do that even before he'd joined the service. He'd been good at assessing people and places and quickly understanding the situation. She'd been proud of her brother, but sad that they had grown apart after he'd left town to join the navy.

"What can I do for you, Mr. Cason?"

"I arrived in town this morning and drove by my sister's house. Imagine my surprise to see my brother-in-law outside mowing the lawn instead of sitting in a jail cell where he belongs."

His words had bite, and she flinched at them. She understood his frustration that Wayne Lassiter was still a free man. She even shared it. She'd had confirmation from Nikki herself that her husband was an abusive, violent man.

"Believe me. No one wants to see Wayne Lassiter in prison more than I do."

"Then what's the problem?"

"Evidence. We don't have enough. Without a body, we have no crime scene, and without a crime scene, we have no case. Everything we have on him is circumstantial, and it's not enough to take to court."

"My sister has been missing for a hundred and

twenty-five days. Are you telling me the police in this town haven't found one shred of evidence to put that monster away?"

"It's not for lack of trying, Mr. Cason."

He rubbed a hand over his weary-looking face. "My sister is missing. She's been missing for months, and no one is doing anything to try to find her?"

"That's not true. This entire community has rallied together to try to locate her. We held searches, and hundreds of people showed up to help. Nikki was loved by a lot of people in Daytonville."

He stood and roamed the room, restless energy pulsing off him like a tiger on the prowl. She'd tried to contact him after Nikki vanished, but the man on the other end of the number she had for him informed her he was out of the country on assignment and could not be reached. What it must have been like for him working on the other side of the world to find his only sister had been missing for months without his knowledge.

"When did you find out?"

"Three weeks ago. It took me until today to make arrangements to get back to the States. My plane landed two hours ago and I drove directly here." He turned to her. "What's being done to investigate Wayne? Are you monitoring his phone calls? Staking him out?"

She was stunned by his sudden change in direction and floundered for an answer. "No—no, we're not doing any of that. We don't have the budget for high-stakes surveillance, and even if we did, we don't have the evidence to support a warrant for one."

He slammed his hand against her desk and she

jumped, suddenly worried about what he might do. He was highly trained and obviously agitated. Was she going to have to worry about him going rogue and taking out Wayne on his own...and how upset would she really be if he did?

However, when he looked at her, she saw sadness gleaming in his green eyes. "I should have been there for her."

She nodded. She felt similarly. She'd known about the abuse Nikki had suffered at Wayne's hands and she'd wanted to help, but Nikki had to be the one to want out, and Melinda had never been able to convince her friend to leave. She'd come close once, until Nikki discovered she was pregnant and insisted on sticking out the marriage for the sake of her child.

"Do you think he killed her?" Noah asked so softly that at first Melinda wasn't certain she'd heard him, but he glanced her way, waiting for her response.

In most cases she would never tell a grieving relative what she really thought if she couldn't back it up with evidence, but this was no ordinary situation. She wasn't looking at this from a legal standpoint where she'd only heard suspicions of abuse in the relationship. She'd had the confirmation from the victim herself, and she got the impression from Noah Cason that he really wanted to know her opinion. "I absolutely believe it," she told him truthfully.

"She deserves better than this. She deserves justice and a proper burial. I need your help to make that happen."

She nodded, suddenly intrigued at the idea of having another set of eyes on the case. The local police had long given up on uncovering additional evidence, and she suspected it had more to do with Wayne Lassiter's friendship with the chief of police than the lack of leads to follow up on.

"I'll do whatever I can to help you. Nikki was my friend and I want justice for her, too. Let me get her file." She reached under her desk for her briefcase. She'd taken the file home with her last night as she often did to peruse it and look for new clues. She pulled out her briefcase, but something stopped her—another image under her desk that caught the corner of her eye. It was pushed farther up under her desk. She reached in and pulled it out. It was a backpack that she didn't recognize.

"What in the world?" she muttered as she set it on her desk. Her mind worked backward, trying to figure out who had been inside her office with a backpack in the past few days. She couldn't think of one person.

"What is it?" Noah asked.

"I don't know. I've never seen this before." She unzipped the main compartment and pulled it open. Her stomach rolled when she spotted electrical wires that clued her in to what was inside the bag.

Noah pushed to his feet. "What's the matter? What is it?" He pulled the backpack open as she backed away from the attached ticking clock and the containers of dark liquid.

Her blood ran cold as she fearfully stuttered out the answer to his question. "It's a bomb."

* * *

All his senses went on alert at the word *bomb*. He rounded the desk and looked inside the bag.

She was right. It was definitely a bomb, most likely homemade. The backpack contained two canisters of a brownish liquid he knew was probably gasoline, with attached batteries for the detonation and a timer. One glance at the timer showed him they had only minutes before it went off.

"Who else is in the building?" he asked as he grabbed her hand and hurried her toward the door.

"I—I don't know. No one. My assistant is gone to lunch and it's Saturday, so most people are off." He saw her glance around the suite. "I don't know. I didn't see anyone else when I came in."

"Run outside. Get clear of the building and call 911. I'm going to make sure no one else is here."

She nodded and ran for the door. He checked his watch. He had only four more minutes until that bomb went off, and hopefully it didn't explode early. He hollered for anyone who could hear him, then quickly ran through the offices, looking for signs of life. He saw none. No one but Melinda Steele was working today.

He hurried outside and saw her on the phone as he cleared the doors. He had no idea how much damage that device could do, but he suspected it would tear apart the inside of the building. He scanned the street. Few people were out and no one was close to the building, but he felt the need to warn them anyway.

"Get down!" he shouted as he sprinted across the

lawn toward Melinda. "There's a bomb in the build-ing!"

People turned at his yelling then screamed and dropped. Melinda spun around as he ran toward her, and he saw the shock on her face as the bomb ignited and fire blew out the windows of the building. It also sent him scuttling to the ground, his back nearly on fire from the heat of the blast, a reminder of how close he'd cut it to making it out safely.

"Get down!" he shouted at her as glass sprayed the lawn and curb. She screamed and dropped to the ground, covering her head just as he did. The smell of fire and gasoline took him back to the embassy where two men had died and he'd nearly suffocated on the black smoke of fire bombs being thrown into buildings. His eight-man team had endured the heat and blind-ing smoke to search for the ambassador and his aide, who were known to be inside, but they'd been too late to help; too late because of political bureaucracy and his own hesitancy to act without orders.

The heat flowing off the building pushed him back to the present, where he crawled toward Melinda, away from the burning structure. Her face was smudged with soot, her soft brown eyes wide with fear. Her clothes and hands were riddled with shards of glass. That would be unpleasant to remove, but at least she was alive. His ears were ringing from the explosion, but he swore he heard the whirl of sirens mixed in with it.

He grabbed her arms and checked her over. "Are you okay?"

She nodded, but she was shaking and tears were

sliding down her face, making trails between the soot and blood. He pulled her into his arms to try to calm her, and she leaned her petite frame into him. She'd had quite a scare, certainly a bigger one than anyone from Daytonville had ever experienced.

"Was there anyone else inside?" she asked him in a small but concerned voice.

"No. No one."

Besides the lack of people, her office had been the only one not dark, something he'd noticed when he'd entered the building only a few minutes earlier. Melinda Steele had been the only person working then… which meant she'd been the target of a bomber.

Melinda clasped her hands together, trying to stop the chill of fear that was inching up her neck. She'd nearly been killed, and would have been had Noah Cason not arrived in her office and intervened. She recalled the feeling of having her feet glued to the floor, unable to move to even save herself. But he'd taken charge of the situation and saved her life.

She glanced up at him now, conversing with the police, probably describing the workings of the bomb to them in the hopes of identifying whoever was behind this attack. Her brain was having trouble grasping the fact that this bomb had been placed beneath her desk. It wasn't a random incident. Its placement had been targeted and precise. After all, it was Saturday, when most government employees were at home, and the building was clear of everyone except for her…and Dawn.

What a blessing her assistant had taken her lunch out of the office today.

She needed to call Dawn. Her phone had been damaged beyond use when the explosion knocked it from her hand and tossed it to the ground. Melinda borrowed an officer's cell phone and dialed Dawn's number. The call went to voice mail, and Melinda left a message. "Hello, Dawn, it's Melinda. There's been an incident at the office. I found a bomb beneath my desk and it went off. I'm fine and no one else was hurt, but I wanted you to know before you arrived back here."

She disconnected the call, then realized she should have suggested Dawn not even return to the office. What was the point? They certainly wouldn't be doing any work today. She didn't know when they would be able to work again. The prosecutor's office in Daytonville had essentially been shut down.

As she watched the fires still burning, she realized all her files were lost, including Nikki's. She could re-order the reports, but the physical evidence that had been stored in the prosecutor's office was now certainly destroyed or at least compromised. Had that been the bomber's intention all along? From the moment she'd seen the mass of wires and canisters, her first thought, her only thought, was that Sean had finally found her and her son. She was tired of running, tired of looking over her shoulder, and beyond ready to put her past behind her. *Lord, when will this end? When will I finally be free of him?*

But she had to admit it was possible this bombing had nothing to do with her except in a prosecutorial role. Had someone tried to blow up the office in order to destroy evidence in their case? Latching on to that scenario comforted her. This had nothing to do with her past. She was certain of it. However, that didn't stop the sudden desire she had to see her son, Ramey, and make sure he was okay. She wasn't scheduled to pick him up until after 4:00 p.m., but she wasn't certain she could wait that long.

She pushed through the crowd and saw Chief Lyle Peterson. "I'd like to go home now," she told him. She didn't want Ramey to see her with dirt and soot all over her, and she'd have just enough time to shower and change first if she left now.

"This is a crime scene, Melinda. You know that. I need you to stay put until we get your statement. I've already spoken to your friend over there. Now I need to hear your side of events."

"If you spoke to Noah, then you already know everything I do. Please, Chief. I need to clean up before I pick up Ramey at the Campbells'. I don't want him to see me this way."

She and the chief weren't always on the best of terms, but he wasn't heartless, and she saw his compassion for her situation. He nodded, agreeing to let her go. "Fine, but I want you in my office ready to give a statement after you get Ramey."

She thanked him then headed for her car. Noah stopped her. "What are you doing?"

She looked up at him. He was also covered in soot and dirt, but it looked surprisingly good on him, especially with his green eyes sparkling. "I need to get my son. I don't want him to see me this way so I'm going home to change."

"That's not a good idea. Someone just tried to kill you, Melinda."

"I'm sure he just wanted to delay or destroy the case, and he succeeded. I doubt I'm still in danger."

"You've got it all worked out in your head, don't you, that it isn't about you?"

"Why would it be? I'm just a small-town prosecutor. I'm nobody." She hated the hysterical sound of her voice, but she couldn't stop it.

His gaze was so intense as he stared at her that she was certain he knew that wasn't the truth. He knew all about her husband and her secret past. "I don't like to hear a woman, any woman, say they're nobody. You are somebody, Melinda. You're an important person to your son."

"Which is why I really want to get to him."

"Fine. I'll go with you. Let's take my car." He turned and started walking away as she stared after him. Who was he to make decisions for her?

"I don't need a chaperone," she insisted.

"I think you just might. Besides, am I right in thinking my sister's file was in that office, as well?" When she nodded, he continued. "All the information on her case is gone. You were her friend as well as the prosecuting attorney, and I'd stake my life that you know everything that was in that file. You've been over it time and time again, looking for some new piece of information that could break her case. That makes you my new best friend and my partner in finding her. Besides, your car isn't actually operational."

She looked at her car, the blown-out windows and the water raining down on it from the fire hoses. He was right. She couldn't drive it, and she didn't have time to wait around for a cab if she wanted to clean up before she picked up Ramey.

He opened the passenger's door to his car, which she noticed he'd parked across the street. She reluctantly slipped inside. He was right. Despite her bravado, she was still scared. She'd convinced herself this bomb had nothing to do with her, but protecting Ramey still had to be her number-one priority. She would help Noah with his sister's case and, in exchange, he would make sure her son was safe from harm. They needed one another. But as he got into the car and headed for her house, she blushed at how easily she'd given in to spending time with this handsome stranger.

He liked the look of Melinda's house. It was a cottage-style home on a quiet cul-de-sac. The cozy porch and Christmas decorations on the lawn welcomed him, and as she unlocked the door, a large Labrador greeted her. She patted the dog's head then motioned Noah inside. He grabbed his overnight bag from the trunk of his car and followed her. The dog seemed friendly, but he knew from experience that dogs were unpredictable. Thankfully, the Lab began rubbing on his leg. He scratched the dog's ear then bent down and petted him, prompting a lick in the face.

Melinda laughed then called off the dog. "Ranger, get down."

The dog did as he was told and hurried across the room to curl up in a doggie bed.

She motioned toward the bathroom down the hall. "You can use this one. I'll use the one in the master bedroom." She disappeared into a back room and closed the door behind her.

It felt good to wash the soot and grime from himself and change into clean clothes. It was like a renewing after the battle, and it always made him feel better. He only wished he could wash off the guilt and shame he felt over his sister's disappearance the same way. His heart had broken when he'd received the news. He should have been here watching out for her instead of halfway around the world.

Again, the sting of failure pinched at him. *Why, God? Why do You keep allowing such terrible things to happen?* He'd been asking that question for most of his life and he still hadn't received an answer.

Once he was finished cleaning up, he waited for Melinda in the living room. A small Christmas tree stood in the corner, decorated with mostly handmade craft ornaments and strings of popcorn. Photographs lined the room of a little boy in different stages of growth, some taken with Melinda and many more without. This must be her son, Ramey. He couldn't help noticing there were no pictures of a husband or father in any of these.

"That's Ramey when he was four years old," she

stated from behind him, referring to the photo he was staring at of her son with a soccer ball.

"He's a handsome boy. How old is he?"

"Thank you. He's six now."

"I notice there are no pictures of his father. Are you divorced?" That was the most likely reason a woman didn't display photos.

"Actually, I'm a widow. My husband died in a boating accident before Ramey was born."

That seemed odd. Widows generally had photographs of their husbands displayed, but Melinda didn't have even one picture that he could see. Still, it wasn't his business. "My condolences."

"Thank you. It was a long time ago." She tugged a strand of hair behind her ear then glanced at the clock. "I told Susan Campbell I would pick up Ramey by four o'clock."

"We should go, then." He led her outside and opened the passenger door for her. She directed him toward the Campbells' home, where he parked at the curb. As she got out of the car, a blond boy rushed out the door and jumped into her outstretched arms.

He enjoyed watching them together. There was no hesitation in the boy's face or actions, nothing like he or Nikki had felt at seeing their folks. They'd never known what mood they would find their mother and father in from day to day, or what imagined slight they might have done to them. On a good day, the yelling and hitting would be minimal, but on a bad day… He pushed away those memories, preferring to focus instead on how happy this child seemed to be to see his mother.

She walked to the door and spoke a few words with a woman—Susan Campbell, no doubt—who handed her a booster seat and a bag. She walked the boy to the car. "Ramey, I'd like you to meet Mr. Cason. He's a friend who's helping me with something. Can you say hello?"

The boy grinned up at Noah, again his face open and welcoming. "Hi, Mr. Cason."

Noah knelt and shook the boy's hand. "It's nice to meet you, Ramey. I've heard a lot about you."

"Are you going to marry my mommy?"

"Ramey!" Her face flushed and she shushed him. "Don't ask things like that."

Noah found himself grinning at such an innocent exchange. "It's okay. Your mom and I are friends, Ramey. That's all."

The boy shrugged and accepted that, then crawled into the back seat of the car as Melinda set up his booster seat and buckled him in.

"I'm sorry," Melinda whispered once he was secured. "He shouldn't be asking that. He's just not used to seeing me with a man."

"No problem," he assured her. He wasn't insulted. In fact, he liked that she didn't parade men in front of her son. He'd been captivated by her beauty from the moment she'd glanced up at him and he'd taken in her narrow face and delicate neck framed by her long, dark hair. But it was the smile that played on her face as she watched him that he'd noticed first. She was quick to smile, and he liked that. Now his opinion of her was growing just from this small exchange. She was a good mom, and that said a lot about her in his eyes.

He stopped that line of thinking before it got out of hand. He couldn't go down that road with Melinda. He'd been through too much, seen too much, to ever deserve a woman like her. What would anyone want with a washed-out Navy SEAL who'd gotten his team-mates killed? He was glad Nikki had befriended her. They'd always dreamed of having a normal life, and it saddened him to know she never got that fairy-tale life she'd longed for. Instead, she'd married a man just like their father, and had paid the ultimate price for it.

Noah had buried himself in work, first as a SEAL and now as an operator for the Security Operations Abroad, acting as covert security for CIA agents in the field. If he could remain busy, he could forget what a tragedy his home life had been, and the dreams of normalcy that never came true.

Melinda met with Chief Peterson later that evening and answered as many questions as she could about finding the backpack containing the device beneath her desk. All she knew for certain was that it hadn't been there before she'd gone to meet her friend Robin for lunch.

"How certain are you that it wasn't under your desk before you left?" he asked her for what seemed like the fifth time.

"Very certain," she reiterated. "I told you that I dropped a pen earlier in the day and it rolled under the desk. I had to crawl under there to retrieve it. The backpack wasn't there."

He jotted a note on his notepad. "What time was that?"

"I'd been at the office for about two hours, so around 11:00 a.m. I left at noon and when I returned, I noticed my door was closed, but the latch wasn't pulled all the way shut. Dawn usually closes and locks it if she leaves the office and I'm not there. I assumed she'd just forgotten or had been in a rush."

"So, Dawn was still at the office when you left it?"

"Yes."

"But she was gone when you returned?"

"That's right."

He made another note then looked up at her. "Did she know where you were going or when you would return?"

"I told her before I left that I would be back by one." She didn't usually have Saturdays kid-free unless she was working, so she'd taken a rare opportunity to meet her friend for an extended girls' lunch. In fact, Robin had been persistent that Melinda take the time to meet her. At first, she'd worried her friend had bad news to share, but their lunch had been about catching up.

"When was the last time you spoke to your assistant?"

She was about to say right after the bombing, then she realized she'd only left a message. "My phone was damaged in the explosion so I borrowed a phone and left her a voice mail telling her what had happened."

"But you haven't spoken to her since you left the office at eleven?"

"That's right. I thought she might call me on my

house phone, but I haven't been there for much time since it happened."

"How did she seem when you left her? Was she nervous? Anxious? Oddly quiet?"

She saw where this line of questioning was going, and she didn't like it one bit. Dawn was a sweet young woman with a bright future ahead of her. Plus, she'd been a great assistant and a friend. Melinda trusted her with her most sensitive materials. "She was fine. Her normal self."

"How often do you make her work on the weekends?"

"When we have a big case coming up. The city won't pay for extra help, but Dawn likes the overtime and they will approve that. Are you suggesting she was the one who placed the bomb in my office?"

"Do you believe she's capable of something like that?"

"Absolutely not. Why would she do something that might put her out of a job?" She couldn't believe they were trying to pin this on Dawn when there was a more likely suspect out there. "Why on earth would you suspect her?"

"Calm down, Melinda. We're not accusing anyone yet, only asking questions. We're also looking at other suspects, such as people you've sent to prison. I have someone tracking down everyone you've prosecuted who was recently released. Do you have any enemies that you know of?"

She shifted in her chair, but hesitated in mentioning Sean. Everyone in town didn't need to know her business. Besides, he was dead and had been for years. "None that I can think of," she stated.

"What about from before you came to Daytonville? Any old boyfriends who might have a grudge against you?"

She shook her head. There had been no one since Sean. She couldn't, she wouldn't, subject her heart to falling in love again. She'd done so with Sean and had been burned by his abuse and betrayal. Instead of being happy when she'd discovered she was pregnant, he'd been furious and demanded she end the pregnancy. His insistence had forced her to make a choice, and she'd chosen to give her child life. In response, Sean had tried to murder them both. How could she ever trust another man again after that?

The chief closed his notebook and stood, indicating the interview was over. "It's a blessing no one was injured or killed, but this is still a very serious crime. If you think of anyone who comes to mind, let us know right away and we'll look into him or her. In the meantime, we'll pull the security tapes and continue canvassing the area."

"Thank you, Chief." Melinda walked out of the interview room with a weary feeling growing inside her. Her entire world had been turned upside down today and she didn't know which direction to turn. She'd known her job could have its dangers, but she'd never witnessed anything more than angry words hurled at her before today.

She stepped into the waiting area and found Noah keeping Ramey occupied with a game of thumb wrestling. She watched Noah let the boy win and smiled as Ramey whooped with laughter.

"Are you done?" Noah asked her, standing to greet her.

"For now. I'm sure there will be more questions later but for now, I just want to go home."

He picked up Ramey, and they were about to walk out when she spotted her boss, District Attorney Jay McAllister, approach her. He was dressed casually in slacks and tennis shoes instead of his usual business suit and tie, but he looked tired and she imagined he had been pulled from his easygoing Saturday afternoon with his kids to the news of the bombing at his office.

He rushed to her side. "Melinda, are you okay? I heard about the bomb."

"I'm fine," she assured him. "This is Noah Cason. He was there when I found the bomb. He saved my life."

Jay reached for Noah's hand and shook it briskly. "Thank you for what you did. I commend you. I'm glad no one was hurt. The police are saying the rest of the building was empty."

"I tried to check all the rooms," Noah told him. "I didn't see or hear anyone else there."

"What are we going to do now?" Melinda asked him.

"I spoke with Judge Nicholson. He's going to postpone our cases for two weeks. That should give us time to put them back together. I'm also having someone go through to see what evidence we had present at our office. If I'm right, we had fourteen active cases with evidence stored at our building. We'll know more once we're finished going through the rubble. For now, go home and hug your kid. We'll deal with all this tomorrow."

"Jay, have you heard from Dawn Littlefield?"

"Your assistant, Dawn? No. Why?"

"I haven't heard from her since she went to lunch. I'm sure she's heard about the bomb by now."

"I expect so. It's been all over the news."

"I just wish she would contact me."

"You don't think she was inside, do you? As far as I know, the fire marshal said no bodies have been found."

"No." Melinda felt silly for expecting Dawn to call her, but she thought she would have at least called to make sure Melinda was all right. It seemed out of character for her to be so aloof after such an occurrence. Of course, she didn't have a phone any more. Maybe Dawn had tried but couldn't get through. Melinda would try to phone her again later. I think you're right. I'm ready to take Ramey home and get some rest."

"That's a good idea. I'll let you know when we've established a new place to work."

"My cell phone was destroyed in the blast. I'll have to buy a new one tomorrow."

"No problem. If you don't hear from me, I'll leave a message for you here at the station."

"Okay."

She let Noah lead her outside as he walked to the car, carrying her son in his arms. Noah was good with Ramey, and she felt like she knew him after all the times she'd listened to Nikki rave about him. But now she wondered at herself. She'd allowed this man into her life and into Ramey's life without hesitation or even checking him out. She'd trusted him completely after the way he'd jumped in to save her. But what did she really know about Noah Cason? And, most important, could she trust him?

Noah dropped Melinda and Ramey at their house and made certain all her locks were secured before he said good-night. He'd enjoyed spending time with Ramey, who seemed like a good kid with a happy disposition, but he was glad when her interview was over and he could drop them at home for the night so he could drive by his sister's house. It was dark now and the lights were on inside. He parked and strolled past the house, observing every detail as surely as he was scouting out a target. In fact, he was. His target was inside at this very moment.

He could see the man between the curtains going about his evening, eating in front of the television, while Noah's sister was out there somewhere in the darkness, alone and discarded. The idea that her supposedly loving husband was lounging on the sofa while watching some sporting event burned him.

Melinda had assured him there had been search parties and community efforts made to find Nikki, but it hadn't been enough. His sister was still missing.

He had no illusions that she would be found alive. Too much time had passed for that, and he'd seen too much during his career to believe that she could have survived this long. Rage bit him, but he tamped back every instinct inside him to bust through that door and beat the truth from his brother-in-law. He hated that he still had the urges for violence, but he supposed it was in his DNA. His parents had been violent people, and he'd inherited their disposition. In his youth he'd embraced those instincts, taking out his frustrations on anyone who'd wronged him. But he'd always felt terrible afterward.

The SEALs had taught him to control that anger and filter it to help people, and it had been a service he'd enjoyed and was good at. He was still good at it even though he'd left the navy for private contract work with the Security Operations Abroad company. Now he used his skills to protect covert CIA operatives abroad. The pay was better, but he'd begun to miss the missions that had made a difference. Every time he'd been called to action in the SEALs, it was for a greater purpose. He'd begun to wonder why God had led him there, away from the SEALs and into private work.

He'd gotten his answer three months ago when the US embassy three miles from the covert CIA base where he was working was overrun by locals bent on death and destruction. He and the other SOA operators assigned there had taken action, rescuing eight American citizens from a brutal attack. But they'd also lost two teammates. He'd been in briefings about the incident when the news about Nikki had finally gotten to him.

He didn't understand how a God he'd placed his love and faith in all those years ago could continue to allow such evil to win. Evil men like his brother-in-law, and the embassy attackers whose only aim had been to kill Americans, then continue to prosper and grow and be rewarded for their efforts. His own government was even sending aid to the very country who'd attacked them and crucifying Noah and his team for their response that night.

He was proud of his teammate Rizzo for his courage in speaking up and telling his story to the press, and he'd heard just as he'd arrived in town that Quinn, another teammate, was joining him in opening up about the attack and their SOA unit's response to it. They'd been told to stand down that night by their supervisor, but how could they? How could anyone sit back and watch others get slaughtered without at least trying to help?

Noah spotted a black SUV with police markings stop in front of Wayne's house. He saw Chief Peterson climb out and meet Wayne with a friendly handshake before walking into the house.

He couldn't help but wonder how well the police department had done their jobs, given that the chief of police was good friends with Wayne. Had they done a thorough search? Had they checked all the boxes in the investigation? Given the determination he'd seen in Melinda's face, he thought she would have made certain they did. At least Nikki had one person in this town on her side.

Daytonville reminded him of the place he and Nikki had grown up in, where the residents had turned their backs on the abuse the Casons had dished out to their children. His sister was innocent, the one innocent in their entire family. All she'd ever wanted was a normal, happy life, but this monster she'd married had ended her dreams. By all that was right and good, he wouldn't allow this evil to win. He would fight it until Wayne Lassiter paid the price for what he'd done to Nikki.

TWO

Melinda fixed a breakfast of eggs and toast for Ramey the next morning, then sent him into his room to dress for church. Her ears were still ringing from the bomb yesterday, but she was determined not to miss. She loved her church, but some days it was hard to get up and go. Today was one of those mornings when the fear and worry of the past threatened to paralyze her. Logic told her Sean had nothing to do with yesterday's bombing, but her fear just wouldn't let it go. After a night of fitful sleep and pressing doubts, she needed to be at church being reassured by God's promise that He had a plan for her life and that one day she would finally be free from her past.

Ramey returned ten minutes later, pulling on a button-up shirt over his Power Rangers T-shirt. She smiled and helped him button it, then grabbed her purse and Bible as a knock on the door announced the cab she'd called to take them to church.

She opened the door, surprised to see Noah standing on her porch. He'd driven them home the night before, clearing the house and making sure the locks were all secured before leaving. This morning he was dressed in jeans, a button-up shirt and boots, and carrying two cups of coffee and a small box.

"Mornin'," he said, his Southern drawl extending the word and dropping the *g*. He was clean-shaven and smelled like a delightful mix of coffee and Old Spice.

"Good morning," she replied, surprised to find she liked the way he carried himself.

He handed her one of the cups. "I wasn't sure how you liked it, so I just got black." She took the coffee he offered. He opened the cardboard box to reveal a half dozen donuts and held it out to Ramey. "These are for you."

Ramey's eyes grew wide and he stared up at her. "Can I, Mommy?"

"Sure, but try not to make a mess."

He pulled out a chocolate-covered one and dug in.

"Thank you for the coffee and donuts, but what are you doing here?"

He frowned at her comment. "Did you forget you promised to help me with Nikki's case?"

"I didn't forget, but I have a lot on my plate right now with the explosion. Nikki's case is only one of several I'm going to have to restructure. Thankfully, most of the files are digitalized so they can be recovered, but the evidence is probably all destroyed. Even if it's not, a good lawyer would argue it's been contaminated by the explosion."

"So that's it? You just give up?"

She saw his frustration and understood it. "No, of

course I'm not giving up, but it's going to take some time to put a case back together." She looked at him and saw the anguish he was suffering. His sister had been missing for months. They'd all gotten past the initial urgency and resigned themselves to the truth. Nikki wasn't coming home. But it must be much harder for him to get there, having only recently learned of her disappearance. For him, it was all so fresh and new.

"I'll tell you what—this afternoon I'll go by the police department. They can print off another copy of the original case file and you can go over their notes. That was the biggest part of my file anyway. At least it's a place to start."

"Why not now? I'll drive you."

"We're on our way to church right now." A car pulled into her driveway. "There's my cab now. We really have to go or we'll be late."

"Why don't I take you, and then we can have lunch and talk about the case?"

"I already have a cab."

He motioned for her to wait then strolled toward the car. He leaned into the window to speak with the driver, then pulled some money from his pocket and handed it over. A moment later the cab backed out of her drive and he hurried back to her.

"Shall we go?" he asked, motioning toward his car.

She had little choice but to go with him. She called to Ramey, and he hurried out the door. She was pleased to see the chocolate from his donut wasn't covering his face and shirt as he hauled his booster seat into the back and she helped him buckle in.

She should be upset with the way Noah had insisted on going with them, but she wasn't. In fact, she found her heart beating an extra step faster as his hand touched her back while he led her to the vehicle then opened the door for her.

Stop it, she commanded herself, forcing the smile she felt coming on to disappear. Yes, he was handsome, but she couldn't go there. She wasn't looking for romance, and she couldn't afford to fall for anyone. How could she ever trust another man? And who would even want her after discovering her hand in her husband's death?

Yet as Noah Cason slid into the seat beside her, she couldn't deny she was glad to be spending the day with the handsome soldier.

Noah was glad Melinda hadn't tried to brush him off. He was intent on getting information about his sister's disappearance, and he needed the details to start coming. He'd already seen some of the news stories online before he'd even arrived in town, but he didn't want half-truths or rumors that the media often gave. He wanted to work off the facts, and he felt certain Melinda knew them with or without her case file. She'd told him Nikki was her friend, and she wanted justice for her. Besides, he didn't like the idea of her going about her business like someone hadn't just tried to kill her yesterday. He understood the danger she was in even if she didn't.

What he wasn't sure of, however, was how he'd talked his way into attending church with her. It was the last thing he'd planned on doing today. He and God weren't exactly on speaking terms as of late. just didn't understand how a loving God could continue to allow evil to prevail. But staying beside Melinda was best for them both. She needed his protection whether she realized it or not, and he needed the information she knew about his sister's case.

He knew he was in trouble when they walked through the doors of the church and found it expertly decorated for Christmas. Melinda dropped Ramey off in the kids' section downstairs, then led Noah into the sanctuary. Several people greeted her, all asking how she was and relating what they'd heard about the bombing. She received them all warmly and introduced Noah as Nikki's brother, who was in town to investigate her disappearance.

Everyone he met expressed sorrow about what had happened to his sister and insisted they prayed for her to be found safe. Outwardly, Noah thanked them, but inside he guarded his heart against their words and sentiment. He couldn't be sucked in by their promises of prayer. He'd found it didn't make a bit of difference in the outcome of anything. He knew because he'd tried it, praying like crazy when he was a kid for the abuse he and Nikki suffered to stop. It hadn't…not until he'd ended it himself with a knife to the old man's back as he was attacking his sister.

He was glad when the music started and they could settle into their seats for the service. He tried to zone out the preacher's words, focusing instead on the atmosphere in the room and telling himself he was just being thorough in protecting Melinda. Yet he caught himself focusing on words like *savior* and *dying to save mankind.* Images flashed through his mind of the attack on the embassy. The chaos of the night had been insane and the gunfire out of control. Those people had cared only about killing. Where had the Savior been then?

Suddenly, he was gasping to catch his breath at the force of the memories spilling back to him. He stood and walked toward the back of the sanctuary, pushing through the double doors, ignoring Melinda's curious stare that surely followed him. He exited through the front doors and leaned into his knees once outside. He needed some air. His throat felt like it was closing up. He did his best to push those memories of the attack away. He had to keep his focus on Nikki now. One crisis at a time was all he could handle.

After several minutes he regained his composure and walked back inside. He stepped through the sanctuary doors and his stomach dropped.

Melinda's seat was empty.

He glanced around, hoping against hope that she'd moved to sit with a friend when he'd left, but he didn't see her anywhere. He hurried back to the row where they'd been sitting. "Do you know where Melinda went?" he asked a woman a few seats away, whispering so as not to disrupt the service.

"She got a note passed to her that she needed to pick up Ramey from the kids' church. She walked out right after you did."

He ran back down the aisle and out of the sanctuary. The kids' church was one floor down, so he headed for the stairs they'd used earlier.

Suddenly, the door slammed shut and Noah heard a scream from inside. When he opened it, a man burst through the door, barreling out of the stairwell and knocking Noah to the floor. His instinct was to chase the man, but he knew he had to make certain Melinda was okay first.

He leaped to his feet and into the stairwell, spotting a figure lying at the bottom. She wasn't moving. Her long, dark hair was spread across the tiled floor, and her face was bloody. He noticed with each step how solid and hard these stairs would be for someone tumbling down them.

He reached the bottom and touched her face. She was breathing normally. He checked for broken bones but found none. She opened one eye and peered up at him, then closed it again and groaned. "Noah, where's Ramey? Where's my son?"

"He's fine," a man who appeared at their side told her. "He's in children's church." He pulled out his phone. "I'll call 911."

Noah glanced around and realized several people had emerged from rooms up and down the hall and were rushing to help.

"What happened?" an older lady asked. "Did she trip?"

He shook his head, anger and shame biting at him for leaving her side even for a moment. "This was no accident. She was pushed."

* * *

Noah paced as the paramedic wrapped Melinda's wrist in an ACE bandage.

"You should really have that x-rayed," she told Melinda. "And you need a CT scan since you lost consciousness."

"Only for a moment."

"You could still have a concussion."

"I feel fine. I'll have someone take me to the ER if that changes."

The paramedic nodded then packed up her stuff and left, leaving Melinda sitting on a bench in the foyer of the church office. Noah had helped her walk to the office when she'd refused to get into the ambulance.

Chief Peterson entered the office, followed by her pastor, Michael Greer.

"Melinda, are you up to telling me what happened?"

"I'll do my best, but I'm not quite sure myself. Someone passed me a note saying I needed to go get Ramey from kids' church. I should have known then something wasn't right."

Pastor Greer nodded. "We use pagers to notify parents, not written notes."

"I know. I guess I wasn't thinking clearly. When I approached the staircase, it was dark, which was odd because all the lights were on earlier. Then someone ran at me from behind the stairwell. I didn't even have time to react before he pushed me."

"Did you see his face?"

"No, it was too dark. The next thing I remember, I was waking up and Noah was hovering over me."

Chief Peterson glanced his way. "What about you? Did you see anything?"

"Yeah. The guy tackled me coming out of the stairwell. I didn't see his face, but he was a big guy, tall and broad-shouldered. He was wearing a baseball cap low over his face. He probably took it off and merged into the crowd. It might have been Wayne."

"Wayne Lassiter?" Chief Peterson asked. "I thought you said you didn't see his face."

"I didn't, but he was built like Wayne."

"So are a lot of people." He turned to the pastor. "Are there security cameras we can view?"

He shook his head. "We have them, but they're not set up yet. Wayne was supposed to install them next week."

"You bought your security system from Wayne Lassiter?"

"We did. He and Nikki have been members here for years."

"So he knows the layout of the church," Noah stated. "And he knew there were no security cameras set up."

"He also set up the camera at the prosecutor's office," Melinda realized. "Did they record anything about who planted the bomb?"

"He sells and maintains security systems. That's his job," the chief insisted. "We have no proof that he was involved in this. You said yourself you didn't see the man's face. Besides, why would Wayne want to hurt you, Melinda? I know you believe he's behind Nikki's disappearance, but even if you're right and he was involved, he's gotten away with it so far. Why would he open himself up to another investigation?"

"Because he knows I'm reopening Nikki's case. He knows I won't give up on it. And he knows I'm the only one who can verify that he regularly beat Nikki."

Chief Peterson rubbed his face. It was obvious he was feeling the pressure to implicate his friend in a crime. "I'll go talk to him and find out where he was this morning."

"He was at church this morning," Pastor Greer offered. "I spoke with him earlier, but I don't recall seeing him in the sanctuary."

Melinda stared at the chief as the details continued to add up. Finally, he nodded. "I'll go speak with him."

As the chief left, she turned to Pastor Greer. "Would you ask Susan Campbell if she will take Ramey home with her for a couple of days?"

"Of course. I'll take care of it," Pastor Greer answered.

As he walked out of the room, Noah looked at her. "Are you sure you want to do that?"

"If someone is targeting me, I don't want Ramey to get caught in the crossfire. Susan Campbell will keep him safe, and he's used to being there. She keeps him frequently for me whenever I'm working a big case and it's not unusual for me to have to leave unexpectedly. He won't be scared by it. If he saw me hurt like this, he would be scared. As much as I want him by my side, I have to make sure he's safe."

"That makes sense. I'll take you home. You need to rest."

She put her hand on his arm. "I don't need rest. I want to do what I promised I would do. I want to help you find Nikki."

He was touched by her gesture, but he wasn't sure she was up for it. "You just had a bad fall. Your head—"

"My head is fine. I promise, if it's too much, I'll stop, but I want to help you."

"I appreciate that." He helped her outside to his rental car then drove to a local copy shop and had a hundred flyers printed up with Nikki's photo on them. He stared at the picture of her. She looked so different in this photograph from the girl he remembered. It had been years since he'd seen her, too long for a brother and sister to be apart.

He was glad Melinda had agreed to go with him to question locals about Nikki's disappearance, because even though she'd said she wasn't a townie and wouldn't be believed, she was still more of an insider than he was. She'd been living and working in this town for years, and even though he might be the brother of someone they all cared about, he was also an outsider.

Plus, he was glad to get Melinda out doing something other than worrying about Dawn. He hated to think she'd been betrayed by someone she cared about, but he'd seen it happen far too many times. He also thought it was probably not the first time it had happened to her. He could tell her heart was guarded. Someone had hurt her in the past. Was she still grieving for a man who'd died so many years ago, or had she taken a chance on love again and gotten raked over the coals? He hated to think so. As far as he could tell, she had a good heart and a caring personality. She was good with her son, and that said a lot about her as a person, in his opinion.

She instructed him to pull into a local convenience store where she said Nikki had stopped nearly every morning for a cup of coffee and a muffin. He pulled over, and they got out and went inside.

As he'd suspected, Melinda knew the man behind the counter. She greeted him by name, and he recognized her easily.

"Good morning, Mr. Hopkins. How are you today?"

"Good morning, Miss Steele. I'm doing well today. And you?"

"Fine, fine. This is Noah Cason. He's Nikki Lassiter's brother. He's in town tracking down leads on his sister's disappearance."

Mr. Hopkins greeted him with a handshake and condolences. "You sister was a very sweet lady. She always had a smile for me when she came in."

"Thank you for saying so. I understand she came in regularly."

"Oh, yes. Almost every morning. She had to have her coffee and a muffin from my wife's baked goods display. She said they tasted a little bit like heaven. We didn't think anything at first when she didn't show up one morning. Things happen. People run late or get sick, so we didn't immediately suspect anything. Although usually if she couldn't stop, she would honk her horn as she drove by. We never saw her that morning, so my wife and I assumed she was sick at home. She'd been looking pale and tired recently."

"Pale and tired?" he echoed. "For how long?"

"Only a few days, maybe a week before she went missing. She claimed she had some late nights grading papers, but she still always had that smile on her face and told us to have a blessed day. She was a very nice lady."

Noah was surprised by how this man's words about Nikki wrenched his heart. He hadn't expected that. Thought he'd built up a defense against the pain and anger of losing her, but everything Mr. Hopkins was saying about her personality rang true. She'd always had a sunny disposition. Even in the dark days when being at home meant living in a nightmare, she'd been a pro at putting on a good face for the world. It was so Nikki.

"Was there anything about her behavior that struck you as odd? Was she doing anything different in the days before she vanished, or purchasing something different?"

He folded his arms and thought back. "She'd stopped buying coffee. Instead, she bought milk to drink with her muffin. The wife and I even speculated that with the paleness and being so tired and not drinking coffee anymore that she might be expecting, but we never saw her again, so we couldn't ask her about it."

His words broke Noah's heart. The change from coffee every morning to milk was a big clue that she'd been pregnant. Being the caring person she was, she would have wanted to do everything to protect her child.

"Did you know about this?" Noah asked Melinda.

She had paled at Mr. Hopkins's words. "She told me the day before she vanished," she whispered, then turned and walked out.

Her words were like a blow to him. He'd lost not only his sister, but a niece or nephew, as well? His jaw clenched as this new information sank in and that urge to lash out grew. Had Wayne killed her when he found out about the pregnancy? He hated to think that way, but how many pregnant women had he heard about disappearing with abusive husbands as the chief suspects? Too many.

But Noah still had questions. "Were there any traffic conditions that morning that would have necessitated her taking a different route? An accident? Road work, maybe?"

"No, nothing. The road was busy, but that's normal in the mornings."

"I'm starting the search for her again. May I place one of these flyers on your door?"

"Yes, yes. Anything we can do."

He thanked Mr. Hopkins for his help.

"I hope you find her," the man said, holding on to his hand. "And then I hope you find who did this to her and make him pay."

There was a bitterness in his voice that Noah recognized from his own anger. The bitterness of someone who'd had something good and sweet ripped from their lives and were angry about it. "I will," he promised. It was one he intended to keep.

He taped the flyer to the door, then waved to Mr. Hopkins and walked outside to the car. He got in as Melinda slipped into the passenger's seat, but he couldn't start the car right away. An overwhelming feeling of gratitude flowed through him that Nikki had had people like Mr. and Mrs. Hopkins in her life who made her smile each day.

Melinda saw his hesitation and reached out for his hand on the gearshift. He turned to her and saw compassion in her lovely face. She was someone who had loved his sister, too, and he was grateful for that.

"She touched a lot of people, didn't she?" he asked, surprised by the crack in his voice when he spoke. He was usually so good about keeping his emotions in check.

Melinda smiled and squeezed his hand in a comforting manner. "She certainly did. She had a lot of friends here in town."

They put up flyers in several other stores, and Noah heard many more stories about his sister's kindness from the people he met. At first, it had made him happy to hear such tales, but after a while it only saddened him. A good person had been taken from this world far too soon, while someone like him had been left alive.

Melinda tensed as Noah turned the car into her driveway, and he saw her flinch. "The gate is open. I left Ranger outside this morning."

He parked then got out and pulled out his cell phone,

shining the flashlight app toward the back of the house. She was right. Her back gate was standing open.

She ran toward it, calling Ranger's name, and Noah followed. He shined the light all over, but the dog was nowhere to be found.

"He's gone," Melinda cried.

"Does he often get out?" Noah asked her.

"Not unless the gate is left open."

He walked to the gate and checked the latch. The lock was broken. Ranger hadn't escaped on his own.

He glanced around, looking for anything else out of the ordinary surrounding her house. He could only think of one reason someone would let the dog run loose, and that was if they were planning to return and didn't want to be noticed by a barking dog…or else they were already there.

He took her hand. "Let's go inside. I want to check the house for intruders." First, he walked to his car, opened the trunk and dug through his bag for his gun. He hadn't planned on having to use it, but he always kept a weapon close by. He'd seen too much evil not to be ready to respond to it if necessary.

He took the keys from her and unlocked the door, raising his gun and flashlight for any unexpected movement inside. Nothing stirred as he swept the light across the living room. He checked each room, making certain to look behind every bureau and inside every closet. Anyplace someone could hide. He was tired of this threat against her and angry that evil men kept causing such chaos in other people's lives. It was his job to seek out evil and eradicate it, but lately he'd felt helpless to do so.

He cleared each room, confident no one was hiding inside. He checked the windows and the back door, making sure everything was secure and hadn't been tampered with. He saw no sign that anyone had tried to break in, but that didn't make him feel better. This felt like a setup for a break-in at a later time, when Melinda would be home alone.

That was not going to happen.

He locked the front door and turned to her. "You shouldn't be here alone. I can stay and sleep on the couch, unless you'd rather go to a hotel."

"No," she said. "I'd rather stay here."

He was glad that was her choice. Going to a hotel would only prolong the danger she was in. If someone tried to get inside tonight, he would be here to catch them. He pulled out his cell phone. "I'm phoning Chief Peterson and asking him to increase security on your street." He spoke to the chief and explained the missing dog and the broken latch. Peterson promised to increase patrols around her neighborhood.

She folded her arms in a protective manner, then sat on the sofa. He could see she was frightened, and she had every right to be. She'd already been through so much, and now it seemed someone was setting her up for attack again.

Noah went and sat beside her, placing his gun on the coffee table and touching her arm softly. "What else can I do?"

She shook her head. "That's Ramey's dog. He's

raised him since he was a puppy. He'll be devastated to learn he's gone."

He glanced at the clock. It was already starting to get dark, but it wouldn't hurt to go out and look. "We'll take my car and drive around the neighborhood. Hopefully, he didn't go far."

She gave him a grateful smile. He locked up the house tight, then they got into the car and drove around, shouting the dog's name from the car's window. Finally, they started knocking on doors, asking if anyone had seen Ranger, but no one had.

As he pulled the car back into her driveway and parked, he could see Melinda was starting to get tired and worried. She'd been through a lot today. "He'll come home," Noah said, trying to reassure her. "If he hasn't by morning, we'll go looking for him again. He must be around somewhere." He reached for her hand and squeezed it, again surprised by how dainty it was in his own. "I'm sure he's fine." Her brown eyes held sadness and worry, and he wished for nothing more at that moment than to wipe it away.

He reached for her face, stroking her cheek, and felt her shudder beneath his touch. Time seemed to stand still, and nothing mattered in that moment except her and the distance between them. She slid into the crook of his shoulder, and he sat back against the seat. He wrapped his arm around her and just held her tight.

She gave a weary sigh. "Thank you," she whispered. "Thank you for being there yesterday and today. If it weren't for you, Noah, my son would have lost a lot more than his dog."

She got out of the car and walked back inside, stopping to plug in the outside Christmas lights that lit up her yard.

He followed her into the house then locked it behind him. She fell onto the couch and groaned. "The past two days have been almost the worst of my life."

He didn't miss the "almost" and wondered what she was referring to. A young widow with a child to raise couldn't have had an easy time of it. Yet she'd still had the time and kindness to befriend his sister.

He glanced around the house again and realized he liked the hominess of it…and he liked her. He wished Nikki had found the kind of happiness Melinda had.

He sat beside her on the couch, uncertain how to broach the difficult subject that was on his mind. "You said you and Nikki were friends. Did she ever confide in you about what her life with Wayne was like?"

She nodded, and he saw the answer he was searching for in her sorrowful face, but he still needed to hear it. She'd already said she believed Wayne had killed Nikki. He wanted to know why she thought it.

"Did he hit her?"

She covered her mouth, and he saw she was holding back emotion. He braced himself for what she was about to tell him.

"He was awful. He was mean and vindictive, and yes, he hit her often. Never in the face, though. He didn't want people talking. But I was taking a spinning class with her at the gym, and I saw the bruises. I talked to her and she opened up to me about what he was like. After that I tried to convince her to leave him. I tried many times, but she was hesitant and afraid."

Her words were like a punch in his gut, but he wasn't surprised. Wasn't the saying that women married men like their fathers? "I'm just now realizing how long it's been since I saw her last. When I close my eyes, I still see the girl I left behind all those years ago. But she wasn't a girl anymore. She was a grown woman with a life of her own." He was surprised by the crack in his voice when he spoke. He was usually so good about keeping his emotions in check. "Did everyone know?"

"She kept that very private. I think she only told me because of my past."

He glanced at her to see what she'd meant by that, and saw her shake her head and turn away like she couldn't believe she'd let that information slip out. Her quiet response spoke volumes—she hadn't seen it only as part of her job. It pained him to realize Melinda also knew the heartache of abuse.

"Was it your husband?"

She squeezed her eyes shut, and for a moment he doubted she was going to acknowledge she'd said anything, but finally she nodded. The lack of photos of him in her home made more sense to him now. She'd probably been relieved when he'd died and finally released her from her dark life.

"I'm very sorry, Melinda." He turned his hand over and clasped her small hand in his. Guilt and shame bristled through him like a wave overpowering him. "I should have been here for her. I should have been here to protect her."

"There was nothing you could have done. I tried to convince her to leave, but she wouldn't hear of it. People who suffer abuse have to make the decision to leave on their own. No one can end the cycle but them."

He knew she was speaking the truth. He'd finally had to step up to his father and face him down, but it had taken years for him to reach that point, years before he'd been big enough and strong enough to take on his own evil monsters and protect Nikki from him. And he'd thought, wrongly, he knew now, that his actions would forever keep her safe.

"Tell me about the day she disappeared."

"When she didn't show up for work that morning, and she hadn't phoned or arranged for a substitute to cover her class, the principal at her school grew worried. She couldn't reach Nikki on her cell phone, so she called Wayne. According to her statement, she says he told her Nikki had left for school hours ago. Later he would tell the police that he'd never actually seen her that morning, only that she was gone when he awoke. Her car was found that afternoon abandoned in front of David End Subdivision. Her purse and the keys were inside, but she was gone."

"Did Peterson even look at Wayne as a suspect?"

"I'm not sure he ever believed it, but he did look at Wayne. He had to. Wayne was the last person to see Nikki the night before, and his prints were found inside her car."

"Is that so unusual? Did he ever drive Nikki's car?"

"No way. He treated himself to a brand-new Charger while Nikki drove a ten-year-old Malibu. He never drove Nikki's car."

He heard the disgust and anger in her voice and felt a camaraderie. She cared about Nikki; she'd been her friend and recognized Wayne's vile behavior as such. He liked that she wasn't fooled by his charm and wit like so many others were. He'd seen men like Wayne before, had even lived with one in his father, a man who could charm the skin off a snake, and he'd learned to recognize real friendliness for the fake mask men like him covered themselves with. Melinda, too, seemed to know the difference, but he'd seen the news and read the touching pieces about the successful businessman whose wife had gone missing, and the press's attempts to make Wayne Lassiter out to be a victim instead of a perpetrator. Not one article or news story he'd seen had uttered any negative remark about Wayne.

"But when her car was found, the seat was pushed all the way back," Melinda said.

"Nikki's only five foot four."

"That's right. I rode with her several times, and I know she always had the seat pushed up close to the steering wheel. When I heard that, I knew something was terribly wrong."

"She wasn't the one who drove it there and abandoned it."

Why had she had to go through that? he wondered. But he knew the answer to his own question. It was because he wasn't there to protect her from it.

His failures continued to compound.

He glanced at Melinda. She'd been a good friend

to Nikki, and he appreciated that. Now someone was after her. He had to protect her. He wouldn't fail again.

Melinda closed her bedroom door, then got ready for bed. She felt better knowing that Noah was sleeping in the den and she wasn't alone in the house. She missed Ramey, but she was still glad he wasn't home. The idea that someone had tried to break into her house had her nerves rattled. She couldn't have him around while she had a target on her back.

Telling him about Nikki's pregnancy had brought up a lot of old feelings. She'd understood Nikki's hesitancy in telling Wayne. She'd felt the same way telling Sean about her pregnancy with Ramey, with similar results. Sean had tried to kill her, and, it seemed, Wayne had succeeded in killing Nikki.

She shuddered at the thought of Sean and Wayne and how similar the two men were…and how different Noah was from them. He was strong without being domineering, and his protectiveness towards both her and his sister was refreshing. She was surprised by how close she'd gotten to Noah in such a short time. She could see herself falling for the handsome former SEAL—so she had to be more careful. She couldn't afford to put her heart out there like that. Someone like Noah wouldn't understand what had happened with Sean. She couldn't believe she'd let it slip that he'd abused her. She hadn't shared that with anyone except Nikki.

Besides, she doubted she could ever fully trust Noah

with her heart. Sean had made sure she would never trust another man again.

Her usual routine at bedtime was to read her Bible then go over casework until late, but tonight she didn't feel like doing either. She changed into her pajamas then fell into bed and went right asleep, losing herself in the hazy fogginess of dreaming, which started out pleasant enough with her and Noah on a picnic, then morphed into Sean pressing her head under the water and her gasping for air. Terror gripped her. She couldn't breathe, and the feeling of being held down seemed so real.

She opened her eyes and knew in a moment it wasn't a dream. She couldn't breathe, couldn't take in any air, and that feeling of something pressing down on her wasn't imagined.

Terror ripped through her. She reached out and felt strong arms pinning her down, and the bed moved at the weight of someone hovering over her. She couldn't scream, couldn't breathe, couldn't do anything but claw and kick at the intruder, though her struggles didn't seem to make him flinch. He was too strong.

Noah! Where was Noah? She had to do something to alert him.

Panic muddled her thinking, but she knew she had to act or she'd be dead.

She stretched out her hand. If she could reach her nightstand and knock something off, perhaps he would hear it. All she could do was fight and pray that Noah heard her and came running.

She flung her hand several times, reaching farther

and farther until it connected with something. She heard the rustle of something hit the floor, and the man above her grunted. He moved, and the weight of whatever was pressing on her released. She pushed it away and gasped for air, her chest and throat aching as she inhaled.

The man moved from the bed. She caught her first glimpse of him from behind. Large, broad shoulders, dark hair poking out from beneath a mask, jeans and boots. The doorknob rattled and he tensed.

"Melinda? Are you okay?" Noah's voice came through the door. He knocked. "Melinda?" He tried the knob again but it was obviously locked, so he knocked once more, the timbre of his voice rising. "Melinda, open the door."

She struggled to move, to run, to form words, but her body would do nothing but suck in precious air. Words formed on her lips but no sound came. Finally, she moved and the man turned. He picked up the lamp from her bedside and brought it down against her head.

Pain ripped through her for only a moment before everything went black.

Noah's heart raced at the sounds from inside Melinda's bedroom. She hadn't responded to him, and he wasn't waiting any longer. He pulled out his gun then kicked in the door. Melinda was lying on the bed, blood pooling on the sheets, and a broken lamp was on the floor beside the bed.

He spun toward the window as movement grabbed his attention. Someone was crawling out, and all he could see was his leg. Noah ran to the window, but the figure was now all the way through. He quickly disappeared around the corner of the house.

Noah hurried to the bed. Melinda was bleeding from the head and was knocked out. He checked for a pulse and found one, thankful for that. He hadn't been too late.

He pulled out his phone and dialed 911. He needed to get Melinda to a hospital fast. As he spoke, he checked the window. How had the intruder gotten into the house without him hearing? He saw marks where the intruder had jimmied the window and crawled inside.

This guy was serious, and he'd done his homework. Not only had he gotten rid of Melinda's dog that might have alerted them to an intruder, but he'd also staked out the house and knew which bedroom was hers. He must have known Noah was in the house, as well, because he'd been sure to be quiet.

Noah heard movement at the window again. He turned and spotted the dark figure tossing something. It broke through the window, hit the floor and shattered, sending flames spurting toward the ceiling. Noah shielded his face and eyes from the shattering glass and fuel. The smell of gasoline filled the room, and the heat from the firebomb was hot and biting. Smoke was quickly filling the room.

He grabbed Melinda, swooping her up into his arms. They had to get out of this room. He'd been in situations like this before, most recently during the embassy attack when he'd been inside a burning building trying to locate the ambassador. He knew how quickly the smoke could overtake a person and how the chemicals in the smoke could affect his vision and perception. Not to mention the damage to both their lungs if they didn't get out of this room and out of the house quickly.

His hands full with her, he pressed his back against the wall and used it as a guide as he moved past the flames. His brain was already feeling the effects. Breathing became harder, and his arms felt like noodles as he struggled to hold on to Melinda.

Smoke flowed through the open door and into the hallway. It was moving fast, and although they were away from the flames, the smoke was still a serious threat. He kept moving until he could see the door ahead of him. He ran for it, then onto the porch and out into the yard. He fell to his knees and placed Melinda gently onto the grass.

His throat burned and his lungs protested as he took in a deep breath, coughing out the smoke and grime he'd just walked through. He touched Melinda's face. She was still breathing, and he was grateful for that.

The roar of sirens rang in his ears, and he had never been happier that help was on the way.

Melinda's house was ablaze, smoke billowing out of the open front door. But at least she was alive and safe for the moment.

But the threat wasn't gone. Someone had already tried to kill her multiple times, and he hadn't yet succeeded.

He would be back.

THREE

Pain was the first thing Melinda realized as consciousness slowly pulled her back. She hurt all over, felt blinding pain in her head and back, and when she tried to breathe in, her throat was raw and sore. She opened her eyes and saw she was in a hospital bed, her arm hooked up to an IV.

Noah was watching the news coverage of the embassy attack on TV. When he heard her move, he clicked off the television and turned to her. His face broke into a wide, handsome smile. He pulled his chair close to the bed and took her hand. "Welcome back."

"How long have I been out?"

"A few hours. How do you feel?"

"Sore. What happened?" Her voice was nothing more than a whisper. It was all she could manage past the scorching rawness of her throat.

"Someone broke into the house and attacked you. He hit you with a lamp. Do you remember that?"

"Vaguely." It hurt to even try to remember, but she recalled waking up to find someone in her room, smothering her with a pillow. She'd fought him off, then he'd attacked her with her own bedside lamp. She grimaced at the memory. She'd never liked that lamp. "Did you catch him?"

"He got away, but not before he set the house on fire. Do you remember that?"

A tear slipped from her eye as the memories came rushing back. All her things, all the years she'd spent making that place a home. "Is it all gone?"

The grim look on his face answered her question. "They tried to contain it, but he used an accelerant. I'm sorry, Melinda."

She didn't even try to stop the tears slipping through. Years of memories, photographs, Ramey's crafts and art projects, gone. Someone must really hate her. "Who is doing this?"

"I didn't get a good look at him. I take it you didn't see his face, either?"

"He was wearing one of those ski caps over his face. All I saw were his eyes." Dark brown eyes, nearly black, and mean. She shuddered at the memory. She hadn't seen eyes like that since the night Sean had tried to kill her.

She gasped, realizing they had looked like Sean's eyes. Only that couldn't be possible. Sean was dead. She had a head wound and she was obviously confused. That was all. It hadn't been Sean in her house tonight. It couldn't have been. Someone was after her and it was a real, live person, not a ghost from her past.

"It's okay. We'll figure this out," Noah said, giving her hand a squeeze.

She liked the feel of his strong grip. This man had saved her life once again. She and Ramey owed him big-time.

She gasped, suddenly realizing she had no idea where her child was. Had he been inside the house? And why hadn't Noah mentioned him?

"Ramey? Where's Ramey?" She gripped his arm, panic robbing her of logical thought.

"He's fine. He's still at the Campbells'. Don't you remember? You asked to have them take him home yesterday?"

Relief rushed through her as that memory returned. He was safe with the Campbells.

"Susan Campbell phoned a while ago. She heard about the fire and wanted to make sure you were okay."

"I want to call him." He handed her his cell phone and she quickly dialed the number for the Campbells. After assuring Susan she was okay, she spoke with Ramey. She was so happy to hear his voice, and her heart finally returned to a steady beat. Yet she hated the concern she heard in her young son's voice.

She tried to calm his worries. "I'm fine, honey. I'll stop by and see you soon. You be good for Mrs. Campbell."

"How is he holding up?" Noah asked when she disconnected the call and handed the phone back to him.

"He's worried about me and he wants to come home, but he's safer there until I know who is behind all of this." She took a deep, steadying breath. She felt better knowing that Ramey hadn't been harmed. She tried to sit up, but the pain in her head sent her sinking back onto the pillows. Still, she had questions that needed to be answered. "Do the police have any leads about who did this?"

"Not yet, but Chief Peterson said he would let us know if they found anything." He pulled a piece of folded paper from his pocket and handed it to her. "He sent over this list of cases you've prosecuted since you've been in Daytonville. He wants you to go over it and see if there's anyone on it who gives you pause— anybody who might have threatened you."

She glanced over the names but couldn't imagine anyone on this list having a reason to target her. She'd only been with the Daytonville District Attorney's office for three years. "I can't imagine anyone on this list who would have a big enough grudge against me to orchestrate something like this."

In fact, she could think of only two people who might want to harm her—Wayne and Sean. Wayne had to be behind these attacks…but maybe, just maybe, it was time to come clean about Sean, if only to hear someone else tell her it was crazy to even consider him a suspect. His body had never been found, but he'd been legally declared deceased, and in seven years she'd heard nothing from him.

She opened her mouth to tell him, but realized there was someone else she hadn't heard from, either, since this all began.

"What's wrong?" Noah asked, seeing her frown.

"I still haven't heard a word from Dawn, and that's not like her. She should have contacted me some way by now. She hasn't come by, has she?"

"No, she hasn't."

"If the Campbells heard about the fire, Dawn would have, too. Even if she didn't contact me after the explosion, she would have now. Something is wrong. I want to go to her apartment and make sure she's okay."

"Of course. We'll go as soon as the doctor releases you."

"When will that be?"

"I don't know. Now that you're no longer unconscious, I'm sure they'll do an evaluation."

"I want to go. I need to see my son. Please go find out."

He squeezed her hand. "I'll go and talk to the nurse."

"Thank you."

"Be right back."

He walked out, leaving the door open. Melinda sat up in the bed. She lay back against the pillows, already feeling better having spoken to Ramey and made a plan to go check on Dawn. But she was ready to get out of here. She needed to get up and find her clothes and change. If they saw she was mobile, then it might encourage the doctor to release her sooner. Either way, she was getting out of here. It broke her heart to have to tell Ramey about the fire and what they'd lost, but she would assure him the most important thing was that they were both safe.

She sat up, her head protesting at the sudden movement. But she pushed through the pain. This was important to her. She pulled the IV from her arm and pulled off the other monitors keeping check on her pulse and blood pressure. She pushed off the bed and stumbled to the chest. Pulling open drawers, she saw they were all empty. She opened the closet, which had several cabinets inside, then opened them and dug through drawers until she found a bag containing her clothes.

She heard someone enter the room and glanced around the curtain. A man in a maintenance uniform was pushing a cleaning cart.

"Just here to collect the trash and sweep up," he told her.

"That's fine," she responded. She pulled out the bag and dumped its contents onto the bed. It only contained her pajamas and they stank of smoke, but they would have to do until she got some more clothes. She supposed she would have to purchase all new clothes due to the fire and smoke damage, which would be extensive. She hated to think of the work wardrobe she would now have to replace—expensive suits for court she'd scrimped and saved to purchase.

Melinda turned to pull the curtain closed so she could change. The maintenance man was gone, but his cart was still there. He must be in the bathroom. She was headed to see when suddenly, he jumped out from behind a partition and grabbed her around the neck. He pulled a knife and pressed it against her throat.

Melinda cried out at the pain. She should have been more alert, aware of him. She hadn't seen a mask, but his cap had been pulled down low, covering his face. Dumb mistake. Maybe her head injury had clouded her judgment. "What—what do you want?" she asked him.

He pressed the knife farther into her neck, and she cried out again. "I want justice," he told her.

"No!" she cried again. She'd survived too much already. She wasn't going down without a fight.

She slung her arms and feet, trying to find something, anything, to grab to fight back with. If only she could make enough noise, maybe Noah would hear it and come back in.

"Settle down," he sneered, pressing the knife into her neck again. She felt something warm run down her neck and knew he'd drawn blood. "Now, we're going to walk out of here real calm-like. No screaming, no alerting anyone, or I'll slice open your throat. Got it?"

He grabbed her arm and moved the knife to her side, pressing hard enough to make her flinch. "Follow me." He pulled her from the room, walking briskly enough that she had to double her steps to keep up. There were no police and no security at her door, only Noah who was occupied at the nurses' station. She willed him to turn around and see what was happening. But by the time her attacker pressed the down button on the elevator, Noah still hadn't seen them.

The elevator dinged and the doors opened. Her attacker pushed her inside. As the doors slid shut, Melinda knew she was in real trouble.

Noah thanked the nurse who'd promised to contact the doctor to exam Melinda and expedite her discharge. He walked back to Melinda's room. It was empty. A custodial cart was there, and her clothes from the bag were spread out on the bed.

He saw blood on the floor, and his heart jerked. Melinda was gone.

He'd turned his back for only a moment, but it had been long enough for someone to waltz in and steal her away.

He ran from the room and called to the nurses' station. "Call security! Melinda's been abducted!"

One of the nurses quickly made the call. Noah spotted another drop of blood on the floor and realized she was leaving a blood trail. The fact that she was bleeding meant he'd already hurt her, but it must not have been badly enough that she couldn't walk. Surely, someone would have noticed him carrying her out of here. But shouldn't they have noticed a woman in a hospital gown walking out too? The blood trail led to the elevators.

He ran to the stairs and down to the first floor, assuming he would want to leave the hospital. He knew he was right when he spotted blood spots on the floor again by the ground floor elevator. He scanned the crowd, trying to find her dark hair in the group. Finally, he spotted her, being pulled along beside a big, burly man in a baseball cap.

"Hey!" Noah hollered, grabbing everyone's attention.

The attacker stopped and turned, too, then took off running, pulling Melinda along beside him. Noah ran after them. They were a good twenty feet from the front sliding doors of the hospital when he spotted the man reach up and pull the fire alarm. People around him began to panic and rush for the front. Melinda became harder to see, but Noah pushed through the people now, all rushing toward the front doors.

He ran through the doors and saw a white van screech to a halt. The side door opened, and they headed for it. Melinda struggled, pulling away from him, trying not to be dragged into the van.

Noah rushed for them. When he was close enough, he tackled them, knocking Melinda free of the man's grip. He and Noah went down, but the man jumped to his feet and dove into the van, which took off before Noah could even get up.

He spun around and saw Melinda on the ground a few feet away. Her neck was cut and bleeding and her knees were scraped, but she seemed to be okay. He helped her up and she fell into his arms, sobs racking her body.

"He was going to kill me, Noah. He had a knife and he was going to kill me."

"He's gone now," Noah assured her. "He's gone."

He cradled Melinda in his arms as he helped her back upstairs. The hospital was still on alert from the false fire alarm, but Noah saw a security guard and informed him of what had happened. He radioed his supervisor, who promised to send someone upstairs to Melinda's hospital room once the fire alarm was confirmed false.

It didn't matter how long they took to get someone up there because Noah wasn't leaving her alone again. He phoned Peterson and informed him of what had happened, and he actually arrived at the hospital as the doctor was finishing stitching up the gash on

Melinda's neck. She'd flinched at the numbing medicine, but now she was calm as he worked. The doctor left the room, and the nurse stayed behind to care for the scrapes on Melinda's knees and elbows.

Noah was thankful a gash on her neck that needed stitches was the worst of her injuries. He'd imagined much worse when he'd seen the blood on the floor.

"Did you get a good look at him?" Peterson asked.

Noah shook his head. "Not at his face. He wore a ball cap down low to hide his face. What about you, Melinda? Did you get a look at him? Was it someone you recognized?"

"I'm not sure," she admitted. "It all happened so fast. He claimed he was a custodian there to take out the trash and sweep up. I didn't really pay that much attention to him. I saw the coveralls, and I believed he was who he said. Then when he grabbed me, I was more focused on the knife at my throat and then my side to really look at him closely. In addition to the cap, he was wearing dark-rimmed glasses, but that's really all I remember about his appearance."

"Did he say anything to you?" Peterson asked.

Her hands shook as she tried to recall the incident. "Yes. He said he wanted justice. I don't know what he meant by that, but that's the only thing he said besides telling me he would kill me if I didn't go with him or if I tried to alert anyone."

"Justice?" Noah said. "That makes me think it's someone you prosecuted, or their family. Someone who believes they or their family member was unjustly convicted."

Peterson nodded. "My thought exactly. Did you have an opportunity to look through that list I gave Noah?"

"I did, but none of the names stood out to me. One more thing about today, though. That van. It had some kind of writing on it, like a decal that had been peeled off. I didn't get a good look, but it seemed familiar."

Peterson nodded. "I'm going downstairs to the security department to look at the hospital surveillance. The camera might have gotten a view of it or possibly a license plate we can follow up on."

"And there was someone else driving the van," Noah said. "I didn't see the person, but someone is definitely working with him."

"Maybe the video captured an image of the driver."

"I want to go with you and look at the footage," Noah stated, then realized he couldn't leave Melinda alone again.

She must have seen his hesitation. "Go ahead," she told him. "I'll be fine."

He started to open his mouth, but the nurse interrupted him. "I'll watch out for her," she told Noah. "I was a nurse in the army. I've seen my share of combat, and I know how to protect myself and her if needed. She won't leave my sight until you return. That's a promise."

He liked knowing the nurse was former military. It gave him the confidence to go.

He followed Peterson and the head of security downstairs to the security office, where monitors were set up capturing video from cameras all over the hospital.

"Play the surveillance video from an hour ago by the

west entrance doors," Peterson said, and Noah watched as the image played.

He saw the attacker pulling Melinda out, then Noah tackling them and the man hopping into the van.

"Stop there," Noah stated as the image of the van came into view. "Melinda was right. Look at the outline on the side of the van. It does look like a decal that's been removed and left behind an impression. But I can't make it out."

"We don't have a good image of the driver, either," Peterson stated. "What about the license plate of the van? Did your cameras capture that?"

He moved the footage a few seconds forward, and Peterson wrote down the plate numbers. Then he took out his phone and dialed his office. "Morris, I need you to run a plate for me. HML 473. I'll wait." He placed his hand over the speaker and spoke to the head of security. "I'll need a copy of this footage."

"No problem," the man stated, then proceeded to make the copies.

Noah stared at the image on the screen, wishing they had a better angle on the van. He could almost see the person in the driver's seat, but not quite. It was frustrating to believe there were people out there who were perfectly fine with helping someone else kidnap and kill a woman. But perhaps this was a family who'd been wronged, and they all wanted justice. Either way, Noah knew this perpetrator had at least one other person helping him.

"Thank you," Peterson said, then disconnected his call. "The van is registered to Danbar Bakery. That's owned by Trey and Robin Danbar. And, get this. Ten minutes ago they called in and reported the van stolen from the alley behind the bakery."

"Robin Danbar? Isn't that the woman Melinda had lunch with just before the bombing at her office?"

"It is. But I've known Robin and Trey for years. I find it hard to believe they could be involved in any of this."

Noah thought he was about to give it the brush-off, but then he continued. "I'll go talk to them."

Noah headed back upstairs, thankful to see nothing bad had occurred in his absence. He thanked the nurse for her assistance.

"My pleasure," she responded. "Your girl here is going to be fine. Those stitches will dissolve in a week or so."

"But when can I leave?" Melinda asked her.

"In a rush, are you?"

"Yes, I am, actually. I want to go see my son and assure him I'm okay."

She nodded. "That's a good reason. The doctor gave you the all-clear, so I'll go get your discharge paperwork."

When she exited the room, Noah turned to Melinda. "Are you sure you want to go?"

"Absolutely. I'm ready to get out of this place now."

He took her hand and held it, guilt washing over him. "I'm sorry, Melinda. I promised to protect you and I didn't. I should have been here when he attacked you."

She pushed aside his apology. "It wasn't your fault, Noah. None of this is. If it wasn't for you, I wouldn't even be here, and I don't mean in the hospital. I mean I wouldn't be alive."

He appreciated her words, but it didn't alleviate the guilt he felt when he spotted the bandage on her neck and knew it was his fault for leaving her alone. "I won't let you down again," he promised her. And that was a promise he meant to keep.

Melinda was released from the hospital with a clean bill of health. But she hadn't wavered in her determination to check on Dawn. First, though, she needed to see her son.

She allowed Noah to help her outside to his rental car. Her head was a little dizzy, but she supposed that was normal after the whack she'd taken to it.

It was unlike Dawn not to contact her, and that worried her even more. She would feel better once she saw her and knew for certain her friend was safe. Jay had told her that no bodies had been found inside the building after the explosion. Why, then, hadn't she called her or come by? After two additional attacks on her life, Dawn's absence was frightening.

They stopped first by the Campbells' house, and Melinda introduced Susan to Noah. She saw the admiration in Susan's face and knew her friend would likely tease her later about a possible romance between Noah and Melinda. She would quickly put a nix on that kind of conversation. Her life was far too busy for romance and after what she'd gone through with Sean, she was still struggling to trust.

She hugged Ramey and assured him she was okay,

despite the cuts and bruises and the bandage on her neck.

"I want to go home," he told her, and Melinda hugged him to her.

She wanted to go home, too, but they no longer had a place to call home. It was nothing but ashes and ruins now. But hopefully, they would be able to recover some of their belongings and start over again in a new home.

She thanked Susan again for keeping Ramey.

"No, please," Susan told her. "It's no problem. Jason loves having him here. Besides, I'm glad he wasn't there when the fire started."

Melinda didn't bother correcting her that it hadn't been a fire as much as a firebombing.

"You need something better to wear," Susan commented, and Melinda didn't argue. She'd borrowed a pair of scrubs from the hospital, but she'd been in only her pajamas when the fire started. She didn't even have any shoes.

She followed Susan to her bedroom and borrowed a pair of blue jeans, a shirt and sneakers. She and Susan shared a lot in common. They were both single moms, widows and thankfully, about the same size in clothes.

Susan also provided her with an extra pair of clothes and a jacket. Melinda was thankful for her friend and gave her a big hug. "Thank you," she told her. "Thank you for everything, but especially for taking such good care of Ramey."

"I'm glad to do it," Susan protested. "Take care of yourself, and let me know if I can do anything else."

"I will."

She kissed Ramey goodbye then walked back out to Noah's car. Now that she knew Ramey was safe, it was time to make sure Dawn was, too.

She gave Noah directions to Dawn's apartment complex, then watched as the town slid past her. This was her home, the place she'd chosen to raise her child, but now it all seemed so foreign to her. Daytonville had its share of petty crime just like any other city, but bombs? Explosions? Murder? It was all so surreal for this little town.

Noah pulled the car into the parking lot and stopped. Melinda got out and glanced around. Dawn's car wasn't here. That didn't bode well. She walked up to the second floor apartment and knocked.

There was no answer, so Melinda searched for a key and found one hidden in a planter. She unlocked the door and pushed it open, calling Dawn's name as she did. Fear rushed through her at what she might find, and she was glad Noah was by her side. She felt him tense as they stepped into the apartment.

"Dawn? It's Melinda. Are you here?" The apartment was neat and tidy—and appeared to be unoccupied. She called again, hoping someone was behind the closed bedroom door. "Hello? Dawn?" No one responded, and Melinda heard no movement. She opened the bedroom door and again saw no one.

Nothing in the apartment gave her any indication whether Dawn had been there recently or not. Had she even returned home since the bombing?

A shiver ran up her spine as she realized something

was really wrong with this situation. Dawn would have contacted her in some way by now if it was possible.

"Maybe her neighbor saw something," Noah suggested, motioning to the door across the way from Dawn's.

Melinda walked out and knocked on the neighbor's door. A young woman holding a baby answered, and Melinda introduced herself. "I'm wondering if you've seen Dawn lately. I haven't been able to contact her."

"No, I haven't, and I was starting to get worried. I heard about the bomb threat at her office."

"Have you seen her or anyone inside the apartment since the day of the bombing?"

She shook her head. "I haven't, but then again—" she motioned to the baby in her arm and the toddler at her feet, who had just wandered over "—I've been pretty busy. She might have been there and I just didn't notice." Her eyes widened. "You don't think something happened to her, do you?"

"I'm sure she's fine," Melinda said, trying to reassure them both. But inside, her fear that something was terribly wrong was growing. "If you do happen to see her, would you have her call me?"

"I will."

Melinda thanked her then pulled Dawn's door shut until it latched. "This doesn't feel right," she told Noah. "This isn't like Dawn at all. I'm very worried."

"Did she have any friends or relatives she might go to?"

"No. She didn't have anybody. Her parents moved to Florida years ago, and as far as I know, she wasn't dating anyone. She was happy to work all the overtime I could give her because she wanted to fly to Florida to see her parents for New Year's."

She hadn't been imagining it. Dawn wasn't here. Dawn wasn't anywhere to be found. She would have contacted Melinda if she'd been able to. "No," she told him. "Something is very wrong. I think Dawn has gone missing."

Chief Peterson sat down and glanced at the report Melinda had made reporting Dawn's disappearance. "When was the last time you saw her?"

"I told you, the morning of the bombing. We were both working. When I left for lunch, she was still there. When I returned, she was gone."

"And you haven't heard from her since then?"

"No. At first I thought it was because my phone was destroyed, but I should have heard from her by now. Her car is also missing. It wasn't in the parking lot at the office, and it's not parked at her apartment, either. In addition, her neighbor hasn't seen her. I worry whoever placed that bomb there might have harmed her." It was an idea she hadn't wanted to consider, but she had to. Dawn had had plenty of time to contact her if she was okay. In this case, her silence was not good news.

"We've already got a Be-On-the-Lookout alert for her car, and we've got her financials and phone records to see if there's been any activity. So far there hasn't been."

"What do you mean you've already checked her financials? Why?" She recalled the questions he'd asked her after the explosion. "You think she's involved in this, don't you?"

He sighed then opened his laptop and pulled up a file. He opened it then turned the laptop around so they could see. Melinda gasped. It was a photo of Dawn leaving the office and getting into her car. A man was with her, getting into the passenger's side.

"We pulled this image from the security feed from the bank across the street. She doesn't appear to be afraid of him. He's on the other side of the vehicle from her. Looks to me like she could have run at any time."

Melinda shook her head, the headache she'd been trying to push away since the hospital now morphing into a knife in her head. She didn't understand this, but it did look like Dawn was leaving with this man of her own volition. She looked closer at the photo. The man's face was hidden by a hat, but he appeared to be the same build as the man who'd attacked her in her home.

It appeared Dawn had betrayed her trust after all.

"Any man who plants a bomb is a killer," Noah said. "If Dawn is involved with this man, she's in danger. He wouldn't leave witnesses."

He was right, of course, and she knew it. This photo suggested that Dawn was with the man who was trying to kill her. Whether she was a willing accomplice or a kidnapped victim, she was in danger.

Melinda shook her head fiercely. She wouldn't believe this until they found more proof. She'd known Dawn for over a year. She'd trusted her with sensitive information about cases. She'd even trusted Dawn to care for Ramey several times when Melinda needed a babysitter.

"I don't believe it. I won't believe it," Melinda insisted. "She's a good person. She wouldn't be a part of something like this. He must have threatened her, forced her to do it. This photograph isn't even that clear. For all we know, he's holding a gun on her."

"We're still investigating all angles," Chief Peterson told her, but he didn't sound convincing. He'd made up his mind about Dawn and her role in the bombing.

He turned to Noah. "On another note, I hope Miss Steele has expressed to you how diligently we've been searching for your sister, Mr. Cason."

"She's assured me you all are doing everything you can to find Nikki."

"Yes, that's true. Sadly, though, all our leads have dried up and our searches found nothing. But Nikki Lassiter was one of our own, and we'll never give up searching for her."

Noah rubbed his head then faced him. "I appreciate that, Chief, but what I am troubled by is why her husband isn't being more thoroughly investigated."

"I can assure you he's being looked at as a person of interest—the spouse always is in cases like this— but there's no evidence to suggest he was involved in her disappearance. I know Wayne. We've been friends for a long while, so believe me when I tell you he's not capable of this."

Noah stood and faced the chief. "I wasn't here for my sister when she was in trouble, but I'm here now, and I'm determined to find out what happened to her. I won't stop until I find her and get justice for her."

"This is still an open case. I can't have you jeopardizing it by going rogue."

"You have a killer on the loose, and now he's targeted Melinda, too. Are you really going to tell me to back off?"

Chief Peterson locked eyes with him again. "There's only one killer in this town, Mr. Cason, and it's not Wayne Lassiter."

Melinda was about to ask him who he was referring to when she saw Noah's jaw flinch. Was he really comparing Noah's service to his country to a cold-blooded killer's deeds?

Noah turned to leave but couldn't resist one last jab before he left. "Looks to me like there isn't much case here to jeopardize." He stomped out of the office and through the bullpen without glancing at anyone, then disappeared through the double doors.

Chief Peterson turned to Melinda. "Be careful around that guy. Wayne says he's got some screws loose in his head. He's dangerous. I wouldn't get too close if I were you."

She followed in Noah's direction, walking through the double doors that led into the hallway. Noah was standing stoically at the window, his arms crossed and his jaw so tight she thought it might break.

As she approached him, he turned to look at her and his face broke into a big grin. The scowl he'd been wearing while talking with Chief Peterson was instantly gone.

"I think that went well," he told her.

She shook her head. "You think that went well? He clearly doesn't like you."

"I don't want him to like me. What I want is for him to tell his good friend Wayne that I'm here in town, and I'm determined to find out what happened to my sister."

"You were playing him?"

"Wayne has been given a pass by this department. I wanted to put some pressure on him, get him worried about what I was looking into. The more nervous he is about me snooping around, the more he's likely to mess up and give something away." He reached for her hand, his countenance changing. "I'm sorry about your friend, too. I hope you're right about her."

"Either way, she's in real danger, isn't she?"

"I'm afraid so."

She thought about Chief Peterson's warning and realized how crazy backward things in this town were. She was trusting a man she'd never met and only heard about from his sister, over the police, but the truth was that she trusted Noah. Perhaps it was because he'd been there and she'd seen him step into action when she'd found the bomb, but she trusted him more than she'd trusted anyone in a very long time, and it felt good.

She could easily fall for this man, but that would be a mistake. They could never have a future together once Noah learned about her past and her hand in her husband's death.

The cell phone salesman couldn't get her new phone set up fast enough for Melinda's liking. She nervously tapped her fingers against the counter as she waited, knowing her nerves were on alert and that was making her irritable with the slow process of replacing her phone.

When he finally handed it over, ready to go, she quickly checked her messages for something from Dawn. Her heart fell when there was nothing.

Noah must have seen her disappointment because he placed his hand on her shoulder. "No news?"

"Nothing."

"The police will find her."

Yes, they were looking for her, but only because they believed she was involved in the bombing of the district attorney's offices. They were searching for a potential suspect instead of a victim, and Melinda feared they would miss something because of it.

"They haven't found Nikki yet." She hated to allow her thinking to go there, but it was true. One woman she cared about had already vanished without a trace. If Wayne was behind the bombing and Dawn's disappearance, who was to say he wouldn't get away with it again?

"Speaking of Nikki, maybe we could go get a cup of coffee and talk about her disappearance?"

She saw his hesitancy to bring it up given everything she'd been through and felt bad for how he'd been rerouted from his mission when he'd first come to town. He'd come here to find out what happened to his sister, not protect her, yet he'd been by her side nearly since the moment he'd arrived in town. "Of course. I believe finding Nikki and putting Wayne away may be the answer to ending these attacks against me."

"Me, too."

She could see he was anxious to get started learning the details about his sister's disappearance. Her phone dinged and she glanced at the screen, noting a text message from Jay McAllister.

"What is it?" Noah asked her.

"It's a message from my boss, Jay. He's arranged for the entire office to work out of a conference room in the public library until other arrangements are made."

"Are you sure that's a good idea? You've been through a lot. Can't you take a sick day or two and rest?"

"My job is important to me, and I have a lot of cases that need to be taken care of." She knew it was hard for him to understand, but besides Ramey, her job was the only thing she had. "I promise we'll talk about Nikki."

"I understand."

She hated the defeated look he tried to hide, and how he'd been derailed from his investigation into his missing sister. "I need to at least go in and get my new laptop. Plus, I've got cases piling up. That two-week postponement won't be enough to recreate all the cases on our desk."

"It's okay, Melinda," he assured her. "I'll drop you off at the library and I'll pick you up when you're done. I only ask one thing. Don't be alone. Make sure you're always surrounded by people."

"I will."

Noah parked in the library parking lot and walked

her inside. Several others from her office were already hard at work at tables set up along the walls as computer technicians were finishing up installations on their new laptops.

She saw Noah's hesitation at leaving her. "I'll be fine," she told him. "I promise I won't be alone."

She found a computer already set up and got to work trying to reconstruct her files. She was having a difficult time concentrating after all that had happened to her over the past few days and didn't really want to be here, but she handled several violent offender cases, and those needed to be prosecuted before violent criminals were placed back on the street for lack of due process.

She was busy rescheduling court dates when Jay entered and motioned toward her. She quickly got up and headed over to him. "What's going on?" she asked him.

"I know you were looking into the Nikki Lassiter missing person's case."

"Yes, she's my friend."

"We've been cataloging boxes of evidence, and I'm afraid hers was one that was damaged by the explosion."

Melinda's heart sank. What little evidence they'd collected was gone. That meant no indictment against Wayne without new evidence, and no arrest. It appeared he was going to get away scot-free with killing his wife.

"I'm sorry," Jay said. "I know how much that case meant to you."

She thanked him then went back to her makeshift

desk. She pulled up the reports from their saved files, but with no physical evidence to back them up, they were useless. As devastated as she was by this news, it would rock Noah. From a legal standpoint, they were essentially starting from scratch on her case. Finding her body was going to be paramount in prosecuting Wayne.

She thought about calling Noah and telling him, but figured she could do so later that evening. She liked the idea of spending time with him, and that surprised her.

"What's that smile for?" a female voice asked.

Melinda glanced up from her computer to see her friend Robin leaning against the table. "Hi. What are you doing here?"

"Danbar Bakery is providing lunch for all of you. Jay phoned this morning and placed the order."

She looked past Robin to see trays of sandwiches and chips being hauled in. "Great, thanks."

"I've been wanting to talk to you for the past couple of days. I couldn't believe what happened after you left me Saturday. When I heard about it on the news, I was devastated. I'm so glad you weren't hurt."

"Thank you, Robin. It wasn't your fault."

"And then to find out my van was used to nearly kidnap you!"

Melinda stopped her. "Wait, what? Your van?"

"Yes, it was stolen right from the alley behind the bakery. Chief Peterson said it was used in a kidnapping attempt this morning. I was shocked! Anyway, I'll let you get back to work. I know you're busy. I'll call you later, okay?"

"Okay." Melinda watched her walk out, but her words had stunned her. She'd thought the van seemed familiar, and now she knew why. The decal that had been removed had been the logo for her friend's shop, Danbar Bakery. Did that mean whoever was trying to abduct her knew about their friendship...or was it simply a coincidence they'd chosen that van to steal?

Ann Massey, another assistant district attorney, approached her table. "Was that Robin Danbar you were talking to?" she asked. "Are you two friends?"

"We are," Melinda replied. "Do you know her?"

"Not personally. Only what I've heard. Her husband is being investigated for bank fraud."

Melinda leaned her elbows against the table. Trey was being investigated? Had Robin failed to mention that? Or was it possible she didn't know? "Where did you hear that?"

"I saw the file on Jay's desk one day when I was turning in a leave request. I know I shouldn't have peeked, and I'm not one to gossip, but the guy teaches my kid's Sunday school class. For all I knew, that file could have contained evidence of child pornography. Anyway, it said a bank examiner was being brought in to look at the bank's records. They suspect he might be laundering money through the bank."

Melinda hated to hear about those accusations. She didn't care for gossip, and Ann wasn't usually one to run her mouth about such things, so Melinda believed what she said. Was that the real reason Robin had been so insistent on them meeting for lunch? Had she been hoping to spill her troubles to Melinda? She wished she had. Melinda would have assured her she wouldn't have to go through such a terrible ordeal alone.

"Have you heard anything from Dawn?" Ann asked her.

Melinda sighed. "No, still nothing. I filed a missing person's report, but I don't think they're all that worried about her. Chief Peterson believes she was involved in the bombing. Can you believe that?"

Ann shook her head. "You never know about some people."

But Melinda was insistent. "I know Dawn wouldn't have done that."

But Ann wasn't convinced. "Melinda, you and I both know from our time working here that people often do things you would never expect. I'd better get back to work. I'm sorry about your friend."

The conversation with Ann had left Melinda's head spinning. She didn't know if she should call Robin and ask her about the charges or not. If she knew and she'd wanted to talk, she'd had the perfect opportunity when they'd met for lunch Saturday.

Melinda tried to get her mind back on work, but it was spinning with all that had happened.

She was packing up to leave when Jay appeared in the door to the conference room again and motioned for her. She got up and walked into the foyer where he was waiting. "Is something wrong?"

"I'm afraid so. Two fishermen just pulled a woman's body out of Lake Barnett."

Melinda gasped. Had they finally found Nikki's body?

"Chief Peterson wants you over there."

She nodded. "I have to call Noah and let him know. We'll head out there together."

"Are you sure that's a good idea? He won't be able to get close, especially since they haven't confirmed the woman's identity?"

"He'll want to be there, regardless."

Jay left her alone and she pulled out her phone. If this was Nikki's body they'd found, they might finally find enough evidence to charge Wayne with her murder. But a tear slipped from her eye as she made the call because, if it was Nikki's body, that meant her friend was truly dead.

By the time they arrived on the east bank of Lake Barnett, Noah's nerves were on full alert. This was the moment everyone had been expecting since the day Nikki had first vanished.

He spotted the blue lights of the police and the red lights of the ambulance before an officer motioned to him to indicate where to park. He stopped next to the patrol car and rolled down the window as Chief Peterson approached the car and leaned down.

"What do we have, Chief?" Melinda asked him in her official prosecutorial voice.

"It's a woman's body, but there's enough damage that it's going to be difficult to determine her identity right away. Dr. Mitchell, the ME, will have to make that call. However, she does appear to have blond hair."

He felt that blow like a punch in the gut. Nikki was a blonde. He put his hands over his face and leaned into the steering wheel as a rush of anger and sadness threatened him.

"We're documenting the scene, but I'd like you to come down and have a look, too."

Melinda sat back in her seat, and a sheet of pale gray colored her face. It was obvious she didn't want to do this, but Noah was glad the chief had offered. He preferred her attention to detail to the police department's, who had botched Nikki's disappearance. "Will you please go?" he asked her.

She nodded, got out and walked with Chief Peterson down to the waterfront. He noticed she stopped several feet away, craning her neck to see the scene despite the fact that Peterson was waving her closer.

The way her body stiffened and the fierceness of her response made him curious, and he wished he could get closer. The condition of the body must be terrible to elicit such a response from her. Surely, she'd seen dead bodies before. Peterson himself had mentioned how she liked to go to crime scenes in order to help prepare for the case to be prosecuted.

Peterson reached for her arm and pulled her closer to the water's edge as he tried showing her something that was hidden from Noah's view. She stiffened again, then slipped and nearly toppled into the water. She dropped to the ground and clawed her way back up the embankment, running back toward the car, her face now flushed and a sickening pallor to her complexion.

"Are you okay?" Noah asked.

"I'll be fine," she told him, leaning into the car as she steadied herself.

"Was it that bad?" His nerves were raw and he wanted answers, but she wasn't giving him any. "Tell me, what did you see?"

She pushed away from him and stumbled toward the crowd gathering behind the police barricades. "I need some fresh air," she said as she walked away. "I'll be fine. I just need a minute."

Peterson walked up behind him and watched as Melinda disappeared into the crowd. Noah turned to him. "What happened back there?"

"I have no idea. This isn't the first time she's witnessed a dead body. She's never had this reaction before."

But Noah suddenly understood perfectly what had upset her so much. "It's the first time she's ever seen a body that belonged to a friend."

Peterson shrugged. "Guess that must be it."

"Do you need me to identify the body?" Noah asked him.

"That's not necessary. Melinda made the identification." He slapped Noah on the back as if to say sorry for your loss. It was kind of touching in a way, and he was sure it was the only sympathy this man would give him.

But whatever the reason or timing, Noah knew one thing. Finding Nikki's body meant a case could now be built against her husband for murder.

Melinda stumbled into the woods, her heart pounding with fear. She'd slipped on the wet dirt and nearly fallen into the water, triggering a panic attack. As she fought to control her breathing and keep her anxiety from exploding into full-on panic, the image of falling into that dark, murky water kept replaying in her head, and the difficulty of fighting to breathe overwhelmed her.

She was back on the boat with Sean, then, in the water with his hand pressing down hard on her. She couldn't surface and she couldn't breathe, but her heart was crying out *why, why* at the terrible act. She hadn't even comprehended at first what was happening to her. She was being held under water by the man she loved, the man who had fathered the child growing inside her, and putting them both in danger. She kicked and struggled, but his grip was too strong, and even then it didn't occur to her that this man she loved actually wanted her dead. It wasn't until one of her kicks loosened his grip and she managed to raise her head enough to gasp for air that she saw him coming for her again, deadly intention in his face. He'd wanted her dead, and he'd wanted their baby dead. Finally, it had sunk in, and she'd fought him as he tried again to accomplish his evil deed.

But she'd had something worth fighting for, and so she had, eventually knocking Sean into the water with her, then watching as blood pooled up around her and he didn't resurface. She'd crawled back into the boat then looked for him again, but still there was nothing, no sign of life and no indication that he was there. Blood on the edge of the boat told her he must have hit it as he fell overboard. She didn't wait around. She'd started the engine and hightailed it out of there, back to solid ground. But what she'd done had been unthinkable. She'd killed her husband.

She'd thought she was past all that, but the fear of plunging into that water tonight had terrified her and forced her to relive that night all over again.

She leaned against a tree as her breath finally began to return to normal. She'd made it out that night, and she'd had her baby and started a new life with him right here in Daytonville. Seven years had passed with no sign of Sean and no indication that he'd ever made it out of that lake alive.

And now she owed Noah an explanation for her actions. How would she ever explain this to him without telling him everything? And she couldn't do that. No one could know the truth about that night and what she'd done to protect herself and Ramey.

She headed back to the scene. She would come up with something to tell him, some tale that she would make sound believable. Maybe she would simply say she was coming down with a stomach bug and leave it at that. Or maybe he wouldn't even care what was wrong with her. His only concern tonight would be wanting to know if it was his sister they'd found in the lake.

She felt sick as the panic began to wash away and the image of her friend's body filled her thoughts. It hadn't been Nikki, but she had recognized the heart tattoo on the shoulder. Dawn had proudly shown it off to her when she'd gotten it.

She was still trying to process what she'd seen when a roaring sound grew closer. She turned to find a set of bright headlights bearing down on her. She screamed and ran, but the vehicle kept coming, following her, swerving as she moved on the road. She darted into a row of trees and felt the brush of metal on her leg as she ran. That was how close the car had come to running her down.

She heard the scraping of the vehicle as it side-swiped the trees and ripped off the bark. She stopped and knelt beside a group of trees and watched as the headlights continued and the roar of the vehicle filled the air, as if calling her name.

I'm coming for you, Melinda. I'm coming for you.

The shouts of the oncoming crowd approaching was music to her ears. The vehicle turned and roared down the road, spewing a cloud of dust and dirt in its wake.

Noah ran into the woods, and she fell into his arms. "I heard you scream. What happened?"

She was shaking as he held her. All the panic and anxiety morphed into tears, and she clung to him, telling him in broken pieces between sobs about her near encounter. "He—tried—t-to…run me—d-down."

"The car? Did you see who it was?'

She could barely shake her head before she burst into sobs again. All she knew at that moment, besides the strong protection of his embrace, was that whoever had placed that bomb in her office wasn't giving up. He'd meant to kill her, and he was still out there.

FOUR

Noah sat with Melinda near the ambulance while the police set up a second crime scene by where she'd nearly been run over.

She had finally stopped shaking, but she still looked so frail and frightened that he couldn't leave her side. Yet he was bursting to know what was happening. No one had told him what they'd seen at the lake. He wanted to know, but he wasn't sure she was up to telling him about it.

"Melinda, the woman that was found...?" She looked up at him, her brown eyes wide with fear. "I'm sorry to have to ask you this, but no one has said anything. The woman that was found. Was it Nikki?"

Of course it was. Peterson had practically said so himself. Why else would Melinda get so upset at seeing the body if it didn't belong to a friend?

She clasped her hands together and sighed. "It wasn't Nikki, but it was someone I knew very well. It was Dawn."

"Your assistant? Melinda, I'm so sorry. When I saw

how upset you were at seeing her, I didn't think of anyone except my sister. Could you tell how she died?"

"She had bruising around her neck. She was strangled."

He glanced around. The police were busy processing two different, but close in proximity, scenes. One group was still working around the body found in the water, while another was processing the scene around where Melinda had been almost run down. Two violent crimes against women in two days. They had to be connected.

"Chief!"

Noah looked up to see an officer hurrying toward Peterson. He handed him a note, which caused a grim look to spread across his face when he read it.

Noah jumped to his feet and rushed over. "What is it?"

"Someone called in an abandoned vehicle three miles up the road. They saw someone jump out and run into the woods. It appears to have damage in the same place as the one that attacked Melinda. I'm heading over there to take a look at it."

"I'm going, too," Noah insisted.

"So am I," Melinda responded, standing.

"I'm not sure that's a good idea," Peterson said.

"I've answered all your questions, and you said yourself I could leave if I wanted. I want to see if it's the same car."

"How will you know? You couldn't even give a description."

"I'll look at the headlights and know."

Peterson must have seen as Noah did that Melinda wasn't going to stay put. He nodded, then they piled into Peterson's cruiser and headed out. A few miles down the road, he pulled over and they got out.

Noah spotted a car pulled over to the side of the road. A lone patrol car was watching it.

"Oh no," Peterson said.

"What is it?" Noah asked, then saw for himself when he got a look at the abandoned vehicle. It was a red Dodge Charger. "Is that…?"

"Yep," Peterson confirmed. "That's Wayne Lassiter's car. I'll run the license plate to be sure but I recognize it as his."

Noah glanced at the vehicle. "There's damage to the bumper that looks like it could have come from trees. No sign of anyone around, or even another vehicle the perpetrator used to get away once he ditched the car?"

The officer guarding the car shook his head. "I haven't seen anyone."

Noah spotted the hesitation in Peterson. "You're still not willing to admit Wayne is targeting her, are you, Chief?"

"I'm headed to Wayne's house now to question him."

"I'm coming with you," Noah insisted.

"That's not necessary."

"No disrespect, Chief, but my sister has been missing for four months, and it looks to me like your office has given Wayne Lassiter a pass. I won't allow the same thing to happen here."

Finally, the chief sighed. "Fine. You can come, but I do the talking." He glanced at Melinda. "I'll have one of my officers drive you back to the station." He looked at Noah. "Are you certain you can trust us to do that?"

"I assume your entire office isn't corrupt. But if anything happens to her, I'll know differently."

He leaned down to face Melinda. "Are you going to be okay?" He wasn't a hundred percent certain he wanted to leave her, but he wasn't going to let Peterson talk to Wayne without him present.

"Yes, I'm fine. Go. I want you there when he confronts Wayne."

He watched her get into a police cruiser and be driven away, hoping he was making the right decision. Peterson motioned him toward his car. "Let's go. Remember, I do the talking."

He wasn't sure he could agree to that, so he kept silent instead. Peterson drove to the house where Nikki had lived for the past four years. His heart tore when he spotted the garden gnomes and birdbath on the lawn, and he knew that was definitely her doing.

Peterson parked at the curb and got out. Noah followed him, anger swelling up in him with each step he took toward the house.

Wayne opened the door at Peterson's knock. He looked relaxed and comfortable…until he spotted Noah. His countenance changed and he frowned.

"What's he doing here?" Wayne demanded.

"He's with me," Peterson declared.

It was the first time he'd seen Wayne in years, and his initial urge was to jump on him and demand to know where Nikki was.

"I'm afraid it's official police business," Peterson continued before Noah could act on his instinct. "Where were you tonight, approximately an hour ago, Wayne?"

He looked at Peterson questioningly but answered him. "Nowhere. I've been home all night."

"What about your car? Did you go anywhere in it?"

"No, I told you. I've been home."

"Did you loan it to anyone?"

Wayne put his hands on his hips and sighed. "No. Lyle, what's this about?"

"Melinda Steele was attacked again tonight. Someone tried to run her down."

"I'm sorry to hear that, but it wasn't me. I've been at home."

"Can anyone verify that?" Noah demanded.

Peterson gave him a look of disdain then turned back to Wayne. "Wayne, your car was found abandoned three miles from the scene of the attack. I ran the plates. It was definitely yours."

"That's impossible. I haven't driven my car all day. It's still parked in the garage." He stepped outside and walked toward the garage, then entered numbers on a keypad. The garage door lifted.

He was the only one surprised when it was empty.

Wayne gasped. "It—it's gone. Someone took my car, Lyle."

"Do you really expect us to believe someone stole your car?" Noah demanded.

"I don't care what you believe, but it's true. It was here last night when I parked it."

"So you're claiming that someone stole your car,

even though you've already stated you were home all day?" Noah gave a disgusted grunt at his excuse.

"I took some sleeping pills earlier. I haven't been sleeping well. He must have taken it then." He looked at Peterson. "Lyle, you know me."

"I'm going to have to ask you to come to the precinct with me, Wayne. We need to sort out some things."

Wayne looked at Peterson, shocked. "I tell you, I had nothing to do with this."

"I still have to ask you to come with me."

Noah thought he was going to balk at the request, but he finally nodded. He lowered the garage door, then followed Peterson to his cruiser.

"Aren't you going to tell him about the body that was found?" Noah asked. He watched Wayne carefully and noticed how he stiffened at the mention of a body.

Peterson sighed. "I was going to wait until we were back at the station."

Wayne turned to him. "You found a body? Was it her?"

"She has a name," Noah insisted.

Wayne ignored him. "Was it my wife?"

"We'll discuss it more at the station," Peterson said, then waited until Wayne got into the car before turning to Noah. "What was that about?"

"I wanted to see his reaction when he heard a body was found. He stiffened. He's afraid it's her."

"Or maybe it was merely shock."

But Noah knew better. He saw fear, not trepidation or relief, in Wayne's eyes. "He killed my sister and he knows where she is. And he knows when we find her body, we'll be here for more than a stolen car."

He rode with them back to the station, noting how Wayne ignored him completely but also how nervous he seemed.

He should be nervous. Because even once he discovered it wasn't Nikki's body they'd found, he'd still be facing charges of trying to kill Melinda.

Melinda stared through the two-way mirror at Wayne as he sat in an interrogation room at the police station. He was calmly playing on his phone as he waited, apparently not worried at all that he was being implicated in attacking her.

She shouldn't be surprised. He'd shown very little remorse when his own wife vanished. And he'd gotten away with that. Why should he worry about an attempted murder charge?

She turned and spotted Noah watching her. This had to be doubly hard on him, knowing that Wayne held the answers to where his sister's body was located but refused to give it up. She could sense the rage building up inside him, but he kept it in check. He had every right to be angry, yet he'd been nothing but kind to her.

She took a seat beside him and wrapped her arm into the crook of his. He was shaking and his muscles were tense, proof that he was doing his best to hold everything he was feeling inside.

"I thought I would be okay," he said, his voice full of emotion. "But when I saw those lawn gnomes in her front yard…" He rubbed his hand over his face. "She always loved those."

Melinda laid her head against his shoulder, knowing there was nothing she could do to comfort him except be there. He'd comforted her during her scares with the bomb, the house fire and the car coming after her, and it felt good to do something to help him.

"Where is Peterson?" Noah asked. "I thought he was going to question Wayne about his car."

"He's letting him sit for a while. It usually helps to shake up the suspect and get him rattled, but it's not working on Wayne. He's just sitting there playing Solitaire on his cell phone."

"You should have heard him, Melinda, trying to claim he'd been home all day but that someone managed to steal his car out of his garage without his knowing it. He was stretching. He killed Nikki, and now he's trying to hurt you, too."

"He must be worried that we're going to find out what he did to her."

"He should be worried." Noah stood and paced, his hands jammed into his pockets and his head low.

She wished she had some comforting words to say. She'd always relied on her faith to get her through tough times, but lately even that had been shaky. Besides, he didn't really look like the "Be still and know that I am God" type. He was used to taking action, and right now his hands were tied.

Finally, Chief Peterson emerged and headed for the interview room.

"I want to be in there when you interrogate him," Noah said.

Peterson shook his head. "I don't think that's a good idea. You two have a volatile enough history already. You'll only make a tense situation even worse."

"He's not tense. He's not worried at all. He knows you're going to give him a pass again."

Chief Peterson grimaced at that jab. "He's not getting a pass, but I do have to have proof that he did something. We've got his car impounded, and it's being searched by my forensics team. My top investigator is going to interview him, not me. He can't fall back on our relationship this time. If he was involved in this, we'll find out."

"If he was involved? You've already convinced yourself he wasn't involved, that someone else stole his car and tried to run down Melinda."

She stood and got between them. "What if he won't admit to anything? Is there any way to prove he was the one driving?"

"We'll take prints to see if there are any besides Wayne's, and we're canvassing the neighbors to see if anyone saw him coming or going in the car all day. The best you can do is wait and let us handle this." He glanced at Noah. "Find her a place to stay and keep an eye on her. I'll call you when I know anything else about Wayne." He walked off and disappeared down the hall.

She turned to Noah. "What should we do now?"

He ran a hand over his face. "I don't know. I guess we find a hotel and hunker down for the night."

"I doubt I'll be able to sleep. I'm too keyed up."

"Me, too." Suddenly, he turned to her. "We don't have to stay here twiddling our thumbs. Why don't we get out and look for your dog? If someone let him out, he may still be around the neighborhood. If we don't find him tonight, we'll check the shelters in the morning."

She liked that idea and nodded. It meant the world to her that he was thinking about something as simple as finding her dog.

Noah and Melinda drove around the neighborhood searching for Ranger. As they passed her house, she grimaced at the burned-out sections and the police tape surrounding her home. She'd lost everything. She wiped away a tear as she let down the window and called out Ranger's name.

Noah reached over and squeezed her hand. "We'll find him. We won't stop until we do."

That dog was the only thing she and Ramey had left. Noah believed someone had intentionally let him out of the fence, and it appeared he'd been right. But hopefully, that was all they'd done to him.

Noah parked at the curb and Melinda got out. She wrapped her arms around her and could see her breath in the cold night air. Christmas lights hung down from where she'd placed them on her house, and her yard ornaments were trampled and broken from firefighters traipsing through her yard.

Noah got out and walked around. "We can't go in

yet. Peterson said tomorrow morning. Maybe you'll be able to salvage some things."

But she couldn't salvage the memories she'd lost. The laughs and the tears they'd shed inside this home.

"How could this happen?" she asked. She didn't understand why this was happening to her. She'd always trusted in God to see her through difficult times, but she had to admit, she was struggling with this. Where was God in all of this? Where was God when she was losing everything she'd built?

Noah wrapped his arms around her and pulled her into a hug. She was grateful he was here for her, more grateful than she cared to admit. She'd sworn never to depend on another man again. She should have learned her lesson with Sean. Men could not be trusted. But when she thought about pulling away from him, she found she didn't want to. She'd only known him a short time, but she'd already become so dependent on him. It should have terrified her, but it excited her in a way she hadn't felt in a very long time.

"Thank you for being here with me," she said, turning to him.

"I'm glad I'm here. I only want to help."

"I know this isn't what you signed up for. You came here searching for Nikki, not to get caught up in my mess."

He gave her a slight smile then touched her cheek, causing a shiver to rush through her. She glanced up at him, into his dark green eyes. Just looking at them made her feel better. His strength and strong presence was the only thing still holding her up…that and her need to be there for Ramey. He must be so scared, not knowing what was happening or what he'd lost in the fire. She shuddered, thinking what might have happened if he'd been home with her, and Noah pulled her to him.

"I'm glad I'm here. I'd hate to think of you going through this all alone."

She touched his face, soaking in the roughness of his facial stubble and the masculine scent of his skin. She'd been alone for so long, but now, because of him, she was no longer on her own, no longer the one who had to be strong and make all the decisions and protect them. She leaned in to kiss him, surprising even herself that she wanted to.

Suddenly, a sound behind him caught her attention. Melinda saw a figure approaching them. She screamed as the man lifted his arm, and she spotted something in his hand. He brought it down, striking Noah as he turned to face the man.

The blow knocked Noah to his knees. The man swung the pipe again and sent Noah reeling. Melinda screamed and ran for the car, but the man grabbed her and pulled her back, shoving her to the ground as he turned back to Noah and pounded him again.

She leaped to her feet and jumped on the man's back, trying to pull him off Noah. He batted her away like a gnat and sent her reeling again to the ground.

Melinda looked up at the man. The shadows hid his face, but he seemed familiar, and the familiarity stunned her. Was she really seeing who she thought she was seeing? She scuttled away as he turned back to Noah and punched him again. She ran into a neighbor's yard and grabbed a baseball bat lying in the grass. She rushed at the man, who turned and grabbed the bat from her, sending her to the ground once again.

Then another sound grabbed her attention—the sound of barking. She spun around and the familiar face of Ranger came racing toward her, his ears back and the wind whipping at his fur. He ran past her and jumped onto the attacker, growling and chomping down on the man. He howled and spun around, fighting off the animal as Ranger attacked. The man turned and ran, and Ranger took chase.

Melinda hurried over to Noah. Blood was on his face and he groaned in pain.

"Are you okay?" she asked him.

"I will be. He caught me off guard."

"I know. Me, too."

Ranger turned and came running back, snuggling up to Melinda. She hugged the dog. He'd not only come back; he'd also saved them.

"That's some dog you've got there," Noah stated.

She patted him. "Yes, he is."

Noah crawled to his feet and leaned against the car. "Did you get a look at the guy who attacked us?"

Her heart was still racing as she glanced down the street where he'd disappeared. "It was dark and the streetlights didn't capture his face." But she had seen him.

Fear rippled through her. It couldn't be him. It just couldn't.

Her husband was dead.

He couldn't have attacked them here tonight.

The blitz attack he'd just sustained was all the proof he needed that he was allowing himself to get entirely too close to Melinda. He'd been distracted and hadn't noticed someone following them or staking out her house, waiting for her to return. However, the attacker had found them. Noah hadn't seen it coming, and that was dangerous. He could have killed them both.

As it was, Melinda was shaken. He could tell by the way she was sitting while waiting for the doctor to give him the all-clear on his injuries. It was nothing but cuts and stitches. He'd suffered plenty worse. She was still trembling with fear even an hour later, and she hadn't let go of Ranger, who'd been given a special pass by the doctor in charge to remain with her while Noah was being treated.

He pressed an ice pack against his eye and motioned toward Ranger. "He's a hero."

She nodded and rubbed the dog's coat. "Yes. Ramey will be happy he came home."

He stared at her. She was beautiful and he couldn't deny his attraction to her, but he would have to learn to push that aside and focus on the matter at hand, namely, protecting her. He was embarrassed, even ashamed, that he'd let his feelings cloud his judgment.

He'd messed up in Libya by hesitating, convincing the guys to wait until official approval for them to go to the embassy. He'd waited too long for that approval, approval that had never come, and because of him, people had died, including two men he'd called friends. Today he'd messed up again.

His life was on a downhill spiral. He'd let down his team who'd depended on him, his sister and now a woman he could see himself falling for. He had to get a grip.

From now on he was hands off, pushing his emotions to the back of his mind. He couldn't focus on them, or on Melinda for anything except keeping her safe. An image had formed in his mind of his sister, beaten and murdered and lying in a slump in the woods somewhere. He kept trying to push it away, but he'd seen too much death. He knew what it looked like, and in his heart, he knew she was dead.

He'd let her down, abandoned her when she'd needed him most. He couldn't let that happen to Melinda and Ramey. They needed him to be his best, and that meant keeping his emotions compartmentalized. She was someone he was protecting and nothing more. She couldn't be anything more if he wanted to keep her alive.

Chief Peterson pulled back the curtain and stared at them both. "What happened?"

"We were attacked outside Melinda's house. He blindsided us."

"You didn't see him? What were you doing?"

He felt himself flush at the question. He'd been about to kiss her. That was why he hadn't seen the attacker approach.

"At least we know it wasn't Wayne. He was still being questioned at the station."

Peterson was right. It hadn't been Wayne who had attacked them. That didn't change his opinion of the man, but that meant there was some unknown person out there targeting Melinda, for some reason they had yet to figure out.

And that just made protecting her all that much harder.

"Did either of you get a look at the guy?" Peterson asked.

Noah nodded. "It was dark but I saw his face. I think I could identify him."

"Good. I'm going to have you work with a sketch artist."

He glanced at Melinda. "Don't worry. We'll find him."

Noah saw the fear reflected in her face, and every instinct inside him wanted to go to her and take her in his arms and comfort her. He couldn't do that for her, but he could find the person behind all this and make him pay.

"I'll come by the precinct once I get Melinda settled at a hotel."

"I know you'd rather not leave her alone, so phone me once you get settled. I'll send the artist to your hotel."

"I appreciate that, Chief. What about Wayne? What's happening with him?"

"Well, we've been questioning him for hours. He still insists his car was stolen, and we've got no evidence to prove otherwise. I'm going to have to release him. I was going to put an officer on detail to watch him, but after this, I'm not sure that's necessary."

"He may not have been the one to attack us tonight, but that doesn't mean he's not involved. Did you ask him anything about Nikki's disappearance?"

"We did. His story hasn't changed about the day she vanished, but when forensics examined his car, they found traces of blood in the trunk. I'm having them tested to see if they match Nikki's blood type."

"Wasn't his car checked previously?"

"No. Nikki's car was examined, but we had no reason to search Wayne's vehicle. Now that it's evidence in another crime, we discovered it while processing the car."

He'd always assumed, as he was sure everyone else had, that if Wayne had killed Nikki, he'd used her car to dispose of her body. Melinda had told him how much Wayne admired his car. Besides, Nikki's car had been the one found abandoned…and the one the police had initially processed.

He shook his head. Was Wayne that clever to have known they would have focused on her car only? He'd allowed the police in to search his home for evidence, but they hadn't focused on his car. Had he fooled them all?

Peterson leaned in. "Even if it turns out to be Nikki's blood, he'd claim the car was stolen. He could claim whoever had it also took Nikki."

Noah glanced at him, surprised not by his comment but by the inflection of his tone. He'd been Wayne's biggest supporter, but now he sounded as if he'd realized Wayne had been involved. "Have you changed your mind about his involvement in my sister's case?"

Peterson rubbed his face. "I don't know. I've been listening to his answers. I had my investigators sprinkle in questions about Nikki. But he keeps repeating the same information word for word. Generally, people who are persistently questioned try to elaborate or provide additional details. They're anxious to find out what happened. Wayne isn't responding in that manner. You might have been right about me, Noah. My relationship with him might have influenced my judgment."

Noah appreciated him saying that, but he wasn't interested in making him beat himself up. "There's nothing wrong with standing up for someone you consider a friend. Let me know when you hear back on those blood results."

"I will. There's something else, too. The autopsy report on Dawn came back. It looks like she died instantly, and we haven't been able to find anything in her background or financials that would indicate she was involved. I believe she was probably just in the wrong place at the wrong time."

He glanced over at Melinda and could see she was glad to hear that. To think someone she cared about had betrayed her would have been an awful burden to bear.

"Thanks for telling us," Noah said. "I'll let you know when we get to the hotel."

Noah was thankful when the doctors finished sewing him up and the nurse brought his discharge papers. It was already late, and he was looking forward to finding a hotel and crashing for the night. Though he still had to meet with the sketch artist before he could sleep.

Melinda insisted on driving, even though Noah assured her he was fine. His head hurt, but the pain wasn't severe, and he didn't believe his coordination was impaired. But he finally relented and climbed into the passenger's seat. He checked an app on his phone and found a local hotel that allowed pets.

An hour later they were checked into the hotel on the south side of town. He'd managed to get adjoining rooms on the fourth floor, and he'd made sure to clear them beforehand. Ranger made himself at home, hopping onto the bed and stretching out.

Noah laughed. "That's some dog you've got there."

She laughed, too, and patted Ranger. "I'll need to feed him. Who knows when the last time he ate was."

"I doubt they sell dog food in the gift shop. We'll just have to order something from room service."

"That's an expensive meal for a dog," she protested, but Noah insisted.

"He deserves it after what he did tonight, coming to our rescue."

She ended up ordering him French fries, and he wolfed them down in minutes.

A knock at Noah's door pulled him away from the dog's antics. He took out his weapon then looked through the peephole to see a man he didn't recognize. "Identify yourself," Noah demanded.

"My name is Carl Adams. Chief Peterson told me to come by for a sketch."

Noah put away his gun and opened the door, shaking Carl's hand and apologizing for his brusqueness.

"No problem," Carl said easily. "You can't be too careful these days, can you?"

Noah pulled the door that separated the rooms closed so Melinda wouldn't be disturbed. He hoped she would get some sleep, but after they were done and Carl produced a suitable sketch of the man who had attacked him, Noah opened the adjoining door and saw she was still awake. Only the dog was sleeping soundly.

"Carl Adams just left," Noah told her. "Do you know him?"

She nodded. "He's a local freelance artist. Chief Peterson uses him whenever he needs a sketch done."

"Well, he did a good job." He handed her his phone, which contained a screenshot of the sketch he'd helped make with Adams. "That's the face of the man who attacked us tonight. Do you recognize him?"

She glanced at the photo, and he felt the change in her. Her face paled and her eyes widened in surprise. Every muscle in her body seemed to tense.

"You do know him. Who is he?"

She pushed the phone back to him and shook her head frantically. "No, it can't be him. It can't be."

"It can't be who?"

She stood and folded her arms, but he could see the fear racing through her. Whoever this was, she had a past with him. He stood and gripped her arms.

"You know this man. Who is he?"

"It can't be him. It can't be."

"Why can't it be him?"

"Because he's dead!" She shouted the words, then clamped her hand over her mouth and began to shake as she sat on the edge of the bed.

A sick feeling raced through him as he sat beside her. "Who is he, Melinda?"

Terror flashed through her eyes as she looked at him, and when she spoke, she was obviously choking back sobs. "His name is Sean Steele. He was my husband."

FIVE

Noah paced the floor between her bed and the TV.

"What do you mean, he's your husband? You told me your husband was dead."

"He is. I mean, he was." She looked up at him, hoping for a little bit of understanding, but she couldn't blame him for being shocked. "I thought he was, but this picture, this is him. I'm sure of it."

"What do you mean, you thought he was? What happened to him?"

She hesitated, hating to delve into the details, but he deserved to know. "Well, he drowned, but they never found his body. He was legally declared dead six months ago."

"And now he's back?"

"It's been seven years and there are some differences around the eyes, but yes, I'm sure that's him."

She knew sketches from memory weren't always reliable, but Noah had done a good job of pegging Sean. He was older, but it was him. She'd suspected as much during the attack, and had spent years looking over her shoulder, waiting for him to come after her, but in truth she hadn't truly believed it. Not until now.

Sean was alive.

And if Sean was in town, he would know all about Ramey.

She leaped to her feet and grabbed Noah's hand. "Ramey. We have to go get him. If this is Sean, he'll go after him."

"You think he would try to nab him?" He must have seen worse fear than that in her face. "He wouldn't hurt his own child, would he?"

The look of horror on her face was enough to propel him out the door, grabbing her hand and their coats.

Noah pulled up at the Campbells' house and they got out. She'd phoned Susan on the drive, and she met them at the door with a sleepy Ramey and his bag.

"Is everything okay?" Susan asked. "It's so late."

"Everything is fine," she said. "I just wanted Ramey with me. Thank you so much for watching him."

"Certainly. He's no problem."

Noah picked up Ramey, carried him to the car and buckled him into his car seat. She loved how gentle he was with him, and Ramey didn't flinch or open an eye as Noah strapped him in.

He carried him again once they got back to the hotel and placed him in the bed in Melinda's room. She covered him up with the blanket, and Ranger hopped on the bed and curled up beside him.

"Thank you," she told Noah. "I feel better having

him with me." She turned to him. "But I'm scared. Am I placing him in danger by having him here?"

He reached for her hand. "If this is your husband after you, he's in danger regardless. It's better he's with us where I can keep an eye on him." He pulled her hand to his lips and kissed it. She was so grateful for Noah being here. What would she do without his strength and assurance?

But she knew she owed him an explanation about Sean.

She walked into the adjoining room and pulled the door behind her, leaving it cracked so she could still hear Ramey if he woke. "I told you Sean died in a boating accident, but that wasn't the whole truth. He was always abusive, but I told myself I deserved what I got. One thing Sean was always adamant about was that he didn't want children. When I got pregnant with Ramey, I thought he would change his mind about wanting a child, but he didn't. He pressured me to end the pregnancy, but I stood my ground. I wanted the baby. Then he seemed to change his mind. He said he was happy about the baby and he wanted us to celebrate. He planned a day for us out on his boat, only when we got out on the lake, he—" she choked over the memory of that terrible day "—he threw me overboard and held me under the water."

She wiped away tears streaming down her face. "I couldn't believe it was happening. I was such a fool to ever believe he would change his mind about anything. But I wanted Ramey. I wanted him so badly, and I knew that he was killing not only me but the baby, too. I fought back. I don't know how I managed it, but I fought him. He must have lost his footing because he slipped and fell overboard. I managed to pull myself back onto the boat, but Sean, he never resurfaced. Not that I stuck around long enough to make sure. I started the boat and got out of there."

Noah looked stunned by her revelation. It was a lot to take in, but she hoped he now understood why she'd kept the details private before.

"Was there a search for him?"

"Of course. I went right to the police and told them what had happened. They searched the lake. They found blood on the bottom of the boat, so they thought he might have hit his head as he fell and either died from that, or it knocked him out and he drowned. For years I thought he might still be alive. I left town but I couldn't leave it behind me. I guess I've been looking over my shoulder for him to appear ever since. But six months ago he was declared legally deceased. I thought, finally, I was free of him." She threw up her hands. "Now this."

He stood and pulled her to him, and she leaned into his strong embrace as if it might be her last. And it might be. She had no idea how Noah would feel about her now that he knew she'd killed her husband…or thought she had killed her husband.

It seemed she was right when he gently pushed her away and walked toward the window. "We've all done things we regret," he told her. "Our priority now is to keep you and Ramey safe. If the man who attacked us is your husband, where has he been all these years? Why wait until now to return?"

She'd been asking herself that same question over and over. Why had he waited seven years to exact his revenge?

"Do you have any photographs of him we could use to compare to the sketch?"

"No, I didn't keep any of his photographs. I didn't want that reminder." Even if she had, they would have been destroyed by the fire.

"I'm sure we can pull up his driver's license photo." He sat down and pulled out his laptop. "Don't worry, Melinda. We'll find him."

She rubbed her head, suddenly remembering the feel of him standing over her as he tried to smother her in her room. Sean was out there, hunting for her and Ramey. She shuddered at the thought.

Her worst nightmare had finally come true.

Melinda's revelation about her husband had stunned him. To think of what she'd gone through made him sick, and to think this man might be back in her life, trying to harm her again, angered him.

He phoned Peterson and asked him to meet him in the hotel lobby. He didn't want to discuss this matter in front of her or Ramey. When he saw the chief, he noticed he looked as tired as Noah felt. None of them had gotten any sleep except Ramey, who had slept through the night and was now awake and as active as a six-year-old could get.

"What do you know about Melinda's husband?" Noah asked Peterson.

"Nothing much. I know he died before she came to town. Why?"

"She recognized the man in the sketch. She thinks it's him."

"What do you mean? He's not dead?"

"Apparently his body was never recovered."

"That doesn't make any sense. If this is her dead husband, where has he been all these years? She's been in Daytonville for four years. Why come back now?"

He'd just hit on the very questions Noah had been asking himself. "I don't know. Can you do some checking around and find out what exactly happened to him? I've been trying to search online, but all I've found are news articles that say he went missing."

"Sure, I'll look into it and let you know. We haven't gotten anywhere with the people she's prosecuted. I think that's a dead end. We should start looking into other suspects, especially if this thing with her dead husband doesn't pan out, which I doubt it will. It's more likely that whoever is after her only reminds her of her husband. Or looks like him a bit."

Noah agreed. "I'll talk to her about it."

He thanked the chief, then watched him get into his cruiser and drive away. Noah hit the gift shop for snacks and headed back upstairs. Passing the indoor pool sign, he got an idea. As he unlocked the door and entered his room, he heard Ramey complaining through the adjoining door that he was bored.

Melinda tried to appease him. "Why don't you toss the ball to Ranger and see if he'll catch it."

"I don't wanna," the boy whined.

"I'm feeling a little tired of being cooped up myself," Noah told them. "Why don't we go swimming?"

Ramey's eyes lit up but Melinda frowned. "It's December. It's too cold for swimming."

"The hotel has an indoor pool."

Ramey jumped up on the bed. "Can we, Mommy? Can we go swimming?"

"We didn't pack any swim shorts."

"That's no problem. He can just wear his shorts."

"We don't have any floaties."

He folded his arms and looked at her. "They sell them at the hotel gift shop. You're coming up with a lot of reasons not to go. Is something wrong?"

She glanced at Ramey and he saw her soften, but it bothered him to think she didn't trust him enough to keep them safe. "I'll make sure it's secure beforehand."

She agreed, but he still saw the reluctance in her face even as she grabbed two towels and followed Noah to the elevator.

Ramey bounced excitedly. Although he was glad to see his mother, it was obvious he was a bundle of energy and a very active kid.

He purchased Ramey a pool float, then they headed to the indoor pool. Melinda clung to Ramey's hand even as the boy pulled to get away and jump in. Thankfully, no one was there so they didn't have to worry about that. They had the pool to themselves. Noah hopped in, letting the cool water rush over him. He turned to Ramey and held out his arms.

"I'll take him."

Still, Melinda clung to his hand.

"Melinda, he'll be okay. I'm a Navy SEAL. I've jumped into oceans. I think I can handle a five-foot-deep swimming pool."

"Mommy, let go," Ramey whined, and she reluctantly released his hand. He ran toward the edge and jumped into Noah's arms without hesitation. Melinda flinched, but Noah caught him.

"Now, have you had any swimming lessons?" he asked.

Ramey shook his head. "No, Mommy won't take me."

"I've been meaning to get to it, but there hasn't been time." Something about her demeanor told Noah that wasn't true. She was afraid.

"Why don't you come in and join us?" he asked.

Her eyes widened, and she instinctively took a step backward. She was frightened. He should have known. Her husband had tried to drown her. It made sense she would be fearful of water ever since.

He couldn't change her mind, but perhaps if he could show her that water didn't have to be something to be feared, it would help her.

He played with Ramey, even teaching him the basics of swimming, and the boy enjoyed the attention and the activity. He felt like Melinda was also starting to relax. She sat on the floor and watched them, and when he heard her laugh, his heart jumped.

"Look, Mommy, I'm swimming!" Ramey hollered.

"That's good, baby! Be careful."

She couldn't help the distress she felt, but she'd allowed Noah to put her son into the water. That was a good sign that she was beginning to trust him.

He swam to the edge of the pool to talk to her. "Come on in. Join us. It'll be fun."

"No, no. I'll just watch."

He reached out for her. "At least put your feet in the water. It feels good."

At his urging, she finally relented. She slipped out of her shoes, walked over and sat on the edge, letting her feet dangle into the pool. He smiled. Another step taken.

"You don't have to be afraid," he told her. "It's only five feet deep."

"I know." She rubbed her arms, and he noticed the chill bumps spreading at something as simple as sitting on the edge.

"Have you always been afraid of the water?"

She looked at him, probably surprised that he'd figured it out. He should have known something was wrong at the lake. She hadn't been so affected at seeing her friend, but at nearly tumbling into the water.

She slowly shook her head. "Not always. I used to swim all the time when I was a kid. I was even a lifeguard one summer." She shivered at a memory. "But now when I get near the water, I just get all panicky. I know it's irrational—"

"Fear usually isn't rational. It doesn't make it any less terrifying."

"I know he can't remember what happened, and I've never talked to him about it. I always made him stay back when his day care or church went swimming, and he always complained that he wanted to go. I kept thinking one day I would get him swimming lessons because I knew I didn't want him to be afraid of the water the way I am."

He turned and looked at Ramey happily splashing in the water. "It doesn't look like he's scared at all."

"I'm not sure if that makes me feel better or worse."

A noise from behind Melinda grabbed his attention, placing him instantly on alert. The ding of the elevator outside the glass-enclosed pool area indicated someone had just gotten off on this floor. He waited, expecting to see a family with a gaggle of kids burst into the pool room and end their private time. But no one came.

He turned and scooped up Ramey. He hopped out of the pool, dropping him at Melinda's feet and picking up his weapon.

"What's the matter?" Melinda asked, suddenly tense and on alert, as well. She wrapped a towel around Ramey and pulled her to him.

"I thought I saw something outside the door. Stay here." He approached the door, gun raised. He pushed it open and glanced down the hallway. It was empty, but the door to the staircase was open.

He heard a scream and spun around. He'd left her side for only a moment, but it was enough. A figure emerged from a storage room and pulled a gun, firing it several times into the glass surrounding the pool. It shattered, spewing glass. Melinda shielded her and

Ramey from the glass. She slipped on water and tumbled backward, falling into the pool. She screamed, a high-pitched, terror-filled cry as she hit the water.

Noah fired back at the intruder, who took off running up the back staircase. He wanted to follow and capture him, but Melinda needed him. He ran into the pool room, glass shards digging into his feet as he ran. Melinda was panicking and taking in water, and she'd fallen into the deep end. He ignored the pain in his feet as he jumped into the pool and grabbed her.

She fought him. She jerked, her arms and legs flailing in terror, making it difficult for him to get a good hold on her. She pulled him under with her several times, surprising him. He'd pulled people from the ocean, but every time the struggle was real as they frantically tried to hold on. He pinned her down and dragged her back, but noticed she'd stopped fighting him. He pulled her from the water and onto the concrete, but she'd swallowed a lot of water and wasn't breathing.

The water hadn't even been that deep...but her fear had obviously been.

No, no, no. *Lord, please don't take her!* The prayer came out of nowhere, but in his frantic state he would take all the help he could get.

He started CPR, his own heart banging against his chest. He couldn't lose her now, and not in something as simple as a hotel swimming pool.

He heard sounds around him and saw someone approach from the corner of his eye.

"What happened?"

Noah recognized the hotel manager's voice.

"Call 911. We need an ambulance and the police here now. Someone was shooting at us."

He ran back upstairs and Noah continued working on Melinda.

Finally, she jerked and coughed up water. Ramey ran to her and Noah sat back on his feet, allowing his heart to slow from the frantic racing it had done.

Thank You, Lord. Thank You.

She was okay, but it had been too close of a call. Whoever had shot at them might still be in the hotel, but he wouldn't take another chance at leaving Melinda and Ramey alone to go look for him.

But Sean, or whoever was after her, had found them. They couldn't stay here any longer.

Noah and Ramey rode to the hospital in the ambulance with Melinda. He and Ramey had some glass shard cuts but were otherwise unharmed, and Melinda seemed to be doing better after her near brush with drowning. The doctors were concerned that she'd lost consciousness, given her previous head traumas, and wanted to keep her overnight for observation.

Noah thought that was a good idea. It would give him time to figure out a place where they could stay without being targets. As she slept, he turned on a cartoon for Ramey, then stepped into the hallway to think. He'd promised her a fun afternoon. Instead, it had turned into a nightmare. He'd let his guard down for only a moment, and she'd nearly paid the price for it.

It wouldn't happen again.

The elevator dinged, and he spotted Peterson heading his way.

"How is Melinda?"

"It was a close call, but she'll be okay. She's resting now."

"We've completed a sweep of the hotel. No one saw a man matching the description you gave me. He must have sneaked out someway."

"It doesn't matter how he got out. He found us. Who did you tell we were staying there?"

Peterson apparently didn't care for his accusation, because he balked at that. "I didn't tell anyone where you were staying."

"Then someone followed you to the hotel."

"I don't think so. It's a small town. People talk."

Noah wanted to believe him. He'd proven himself by admitting his mistakes about Wayne and taking measures to correct it. Besides, he was their only ally in this…at least, the only one Noah really trusted. "I'm sorry. I'm just a little rattled."

"It's understandable. Look, Noah, I'm on your side. I want to find whoever is after Melinda and stop him."

"Thanks. We appreciate your help. They're keeping Melinda overnight. Ramey and I can sleep on the pull-out sofa. We'll be fine for tonight, but we're going to need somewhere else to go. I don't know this town like you do, but we need to find someplace no one knows about."

"My sister is a Realtor. I'll call her. She may know of a house to rent where you can lie low."

Noah pressed him further. "No one can know. No one."

"I won't tell anyone, Noah."

"Not your wife, not your officers, no one."

He nodded, understanding completely. "No one else needs to know." He pulled out his phone. "I'll make the call."

Noah thanked him, then watched him walk away. He stepped back into the room. Melinda was still sleeping on the bed, and Ramey was quietly watching TV. His heart was overwhelmed with the need to protect these two people. They'd become so important to him in such a short time.

But he felt doubt wiggling its way through him. Did he have what it took to keep them both safe? He'd failed too many times already. He couldn't let someone he cared about down again.

Noah drove them east of town and turned off onto a lake road. He drove up a hill to the very top, where a large cabin sat overlooking the lake and other houses. It was secluded and very private.

"You should be safe here," he stated, getting out of the car and glancing around. "No one will be able to approach the house without us knowing, and you'd have to know where this place is in order to find it."

She had to agree. The house was surrounded by woods, and she was certain it would have been a beautiful place to vacation if she wasn't fighting for her life.

She unbuckled Ramey and let Ranger run loose. Ramey went chasing after him. She ushered them both into the house and looked around at her new surround-ings. The high ceilings, feature fireplace and modern kitchen made this the perfect place for a romantic get-away, but who would ever think to look for her here?

"How did you find this place?" she asked Noah.

"Peterson's sister is a Realtor. It's being rented out by the company she works for."

She still wasn't sure about Chief Peterson. "How do you know we can trust him after what happened with Wayne?"

Noah glanced her way. "I think he's been shaken up by all this, but he's proven he's trustworthy. He sees Wayne for what he is now. Besides, I'm not sure we have much choice in the matter. He's the only one on our side."

"At least there's plenty of room for Ramey and Ranger to run around." She pointed toward a door. "We'll take this bedroom."

"Take whichever one you want. I'll be on the couch so I can keep my ears open. But once we're settled, we should talk."

"About what?"

"I know you're convinced this is your husband who's after you, but we should also look into other suspects. I want to go back through the day of the bombing."

"Okay." She joined him at the table and pulled out a chair. "What about it?"

"You were working on a Saturday. Who else knew you were going to be doing that?"

She tried to think back. "Dawn, obviously. I'd cleared it with my boss, Jay McAllister. Susan Campbell. Honestly, anyone could have suspected. I've been doing it practically since Nikki vanished. Everyone knows I've been trying to pin her disappearance on Wayne. It's common knowledge. Even my friend Robin had to convince me to have lunch with her that day."

"What do you mean she had to convince you?"

"She'd been on me for a while to get together. Said I was putting too much on my shoulders. That I needed to let this go." A tear slipped from her eye as she thought about Robin's glib attitude over Nikki's disappearance. She'd told Melinda to give up searching for the truth about her disappearance. Although after a few months, that had seemed to be the opinion of most around town. Nikki's case had vanished from their minds.

"Who knew you were going to lunch with Robin?"

"I don't know. Not many people. She'd been calling me all week trying to pin it down, but I'd resisted, claiming I wanted to stay at the office and work. Finally, Friday night, I agreed to meet with her at lunch, but only for a short time. I didn't really want to go, but I realized she was right. I'd been devoting all my time to finding Nikki and not spending any time with my other friends."

"So then how did the bomber know when you'd be gone from the office so he could plant the bomb? If we're assuming it wasn't Dawn who told him, maybe it was Robin?"

She choked over the shock of that statement. "Robin Danbar? She goes to my church. Why would she be involved with someone like that?"

"I don't know. That's what we're trying to figure out. You said she was adamant about you going to lunch with her all week."

"Yes. No." She didn't like the way he was accusing her friends of wrongdoing. "She wanted us to meet Saturday afternoon. Even when she called me at the beginning of the week, she wanted to meet on Saturday at noon at Main Street Café. She said it was the only time she could get away, and we should think of it as stealing an hour or so from our hectic lives."

"Did you already know Ramey was going with the Campbells and you wouldn't have him? Or was that spur of the moment?"

"They'd been planning on going to an outing at the zoo for several weeks now. I knew Ramey wouldn't be home so I thought I'd be able to get a lot of work done." She glanced up at him, a terrible feeling rumbling through her. "Do you think someone knew Ramey would be gone?"

"I'm thinking whoever is doing this seems to know a lot about you, Melinda. Where you go and when. It all points to someone close to you."

She laughed. "It's a small town. Everyone knows everything."

He remembered that being true. Everyone knew. No one said a word. "Where is this restaurant you went to?"

"Around the corner from my office."

"Do you have to have reservations to eat there?"

"No, of course not. Especially not on a Saturday afternoon. Why?"

"I was just wondering if there was a way to determine how long she had been planning this get-together."

"Robin has been my friend for years. She and her husband, Trey, go to my church. She has a bakery downtown where she sells cakes and cookies and pastries. Trust me, she's no criminal."

He shook his head. "I don't think you understand how much danger you're in, Melinda. Someone has tried to kill you more than once. He'll try again, and his actions seem to indicate that he knows all about your comings and goings. He specifically targeted your office at a time when no one but you would be there. He doesn't want to take down the district attorney's office. He wants to take down *you*. Which means we need to delve into your life with a fine-tooth comb until we discover the reason someone wants you dead, and how he's gotten so much information about you."

His words had been harsh, but he was right. Someone was targeting her, and until they knew differently, everyone was a suspect.

"Now, tell me about Robin. You said she owns a bakery downtown? What does her husband do?"

"He's the bank manager at First National. He's been there for years. Apparently, he started out as a teller and worked his way up the ladder through the years. Robin talks about it all the time. She's very proud of him. He also helps her out at the bakery whenever he can."

"Who else is close to you?"

She thought about the people she saw daily. It wasn't a big list. "Aside from Dawn, Susan Campbell is the closest person in our life. She watches Ramey for me whenever I need the help. She's always been there for us."

"Tell me about her. Is she married?"

"She was. Her husband died from cancer two years ago."

"What does she do?"

"She has a son named Jason, who is two years younger than Ramey. He hasn't started school yet, so she stays home with him. She lives off her husband's pension and social security checks. She's always quick to offer to help with Ramey whenever I need it. Honestly, I don't know what I would do without her some days."

"Who else?"

She struggled to come up with any more names. She was a private person, and she and Ramey stayed pretty much to themselves, especially since Nikki had vanished.

But Noah wasn't letting her off the hook. "Who else? Do you have a gardener? Someone you speak to at the grocery store? Coworkers? Come on, Melinda, there has to be someone who sticks out to you."

"No, there's isn't. Not that I've noticed." Fear welled up inside her. There was an entire town of suspects, people she'd trusted for years and called her neighbors, but she had to admit she didn't really know any of them. She'd kept herself too guarded, afraid of being hurt again. "I'm sorry, Noah. I just don't know."

His face softened, and he knelt beside her and held her hand. "I'm sorry. I was pushing too hard."

"I find it hard to wrap my head around the fact that someone in this town wants me dead. It's Sean. I'm certain of it."

"You said the sketch looked different. Don't you think it could have been someone else?"

"It's been seven years. He looked older, harder, but the facial features were the same. It was him, Noah, or else someone who looks like him."

"I asked Chief Peterson to pull the file on his death. As soon as he gets it, we'll look it over and see if there's any possibility it could be him. In the meantime, we should keep looking, because even if it turns out to be Sean, he knows an awful lot about your life. Where and when you work, where you go to church. Either he's following you around, disguised as someone else, or someone is telling him everything about you. Either way, we need to find out."

She put her face in her hands and tried to push back the tears that threatened to explode. She'd chosen this town as a safe haven for her and Ramey, and now all that was ruined. She wanted to scream and yell at the world. When would the terribleness stop? When would she ever be free from her past?

"Mommy, are you crying?" Ramey's voice surprised her. She'd thought he was playing in the bedroom with Ranger. She quickly dried her eyes, but before she could answer, Noah stood and went to him.

"No, buddy. Your mom is just sad because there are no Christmas decorations in this house. What do you say we string some lights and make this place a little more festive?"

Ramey clapped his hands and jumped up and down. "Yes!"

Melinda couldn't help but smile at their interaction. "How do you know there are any Christmas lights in this house?" she asked Noah.

He looked at her and shrugged. "I guess I don't. We'll just have to buy some. And maybe we'll stop by that bakery your friend owns and get some cupcakes while we're out."

Ramey jumped up and down, hollering and hooting. He loved cupcakes, although she doubted sugar was what he needed while cooped up inside. He was already energetic enough. But Noah's suggestion about stopping by the bakery wasn't lost on her. He wasn't only after cupcakes. He wanted to question Robin and Trey.

"Is it safe?" Melinda asked, and Noah looked at her, his green eyes intense with determination.

"We won't find the answers we need if we stay here. I think we'll be safe. We'll be on the street surrounded by people. And we'll take several different routes to make certain no one knows where we came from or follows us back here."

She got up and helped Ramey pull on his coat and gloves. If Noah felt the need to question her friends, then she wasn't going to get in his way. She wasn't staying behind, either. No one may know about this safe house, but someone had managed to find them once before, and she wasn't going to chance being alone if it happened again.

No matter where they went, she was safer with Noah by her side.

SIX

A twenty-foot Christmas tree sat in the middle of downtown, decorated and illuminated against a clear night sky. Ramey's eyes sparkled as they walked down Main Street and he eyed all the Christmas spectacle. Garland hung from the buildings, and net lighting covered the street. Daytonville had a busy downtown, with cafés and shops and even a dollar store where Noah purchased several strands of lights for the house. Maybe they couldn't go all out with the decorations, but Melinda was glad Ramey would have something to remind him it was Christmas.

For a moment she forgot the danger they were in and basked in the glow of the downtown spirit. Music was playing through speakers along the street, and people were in and out of shops and visiting. It struck her as something right out of a magazine, and she was just another patron strolling along Main Street with her son and beau. She knew it was silly, but as she and Noah walked hand in hand, she could almost imagine a future with the handsome SEAL. But even on a night like this, when everything seemed right with the world, she wasn't ready to fully commit her heart to anyone, even Noah.

He led her toward the bakery and held the door for her, a reminder that they weren't really a happy little family as she'd imagined. They were there on a mission to interrogate her friends. A part of her hoped Robin and Trey wouldn't even be here. That they'd handed off the bakery's duties to one of their employees for the night, but then Noah would only insist on returning at another time. It was better to get this over with as soon and as easily as possible.

"Melinda!" Robin spotted her and called to her the moment they stepped inside. She hurried from behind the counter and pulled Melinda into a hug. "How are you?" she asked, her voice full of distress. "I heard about Dawn. I'm just sick about all that's happened to you. You must be devastated."

"It hasn't been easy. Thankfully, I've had Noah to look out for me." She turned to him and made the introductions. "This is Noah Cason. He's Nikki's brother. He came to town to look into her disappearance, but it seems he's gotten caught up in all this with us."

Robin held out her hand, and Noah shook it. "It's nice to meet you, Noah. I'm very sorry about your sister."

"Thank you. Is there someplace we can talk privately? And is your husband here?"

She glanced at Melinda questioningly, then nodded. "Sure, let's go to the back. Trey is there now working on the books." She turned to one of her employees.

"Beth, would you let Ramey pick out a cupcake then take him to the break room?"

"Sure," Beth stated. She took Ramey's hand and he went with her willingly, his mind already preoccupied with the lure of a cupcake.

"Don't worry. You'll be able to see him in the break room from the office," Robin told her. "I know how you fret."

They followed Robin through the kitchen toward the back of the building. "The office is too small for us all to fit. Wait here while I get Trey."

She was gone only moments, then returned with her husband following behind her. He stepped out and greeted Noah, then hugged Melinda. It had been a while since she'd seen him, and Melinda noticed he looked thinner than he had been the last time.

"What's going on?" he asked, surprised by their sudden request for a meeting.

Noah took charge, and Melinda let him. She didn't want her friends to think she didn't trust them, but she recognized that Noah needed to follow his gut and flesh out any leads he could find. She wasn't totally against it, either. He was right when he'd said Sean seemed to know a lot about her life. Too much, in fact. How had he gotten so close to her without her realizing it? She shuddered at the thought of him being out there watching her.

"You're aware of the attacks against Melinda. We're following up on the events leading up to the first attack, the bombing at her office. She told me she was having lunch with you, Robin, that afternoon."

"Yes, that's right. We had lunch at Main Street Café. If only I could have convinced you to stay longer, Melinda, then you wouldn't have been in any danger. But thankfully, Noah was there to pull you out."

"I've been thanking him quite a bit lately," Melinda admitted.

"Melinda said you seemed adamant about her meeting you at noon. Why was that?"

She glanced his way, then at Melinda, confusion pooling in her eyes. "I'm not sure what you mean."

"Only that you kept repeating Saturday at noon. Why did it have to be then?"

She glanced at her husband, finally appearing to understand that she was being questioned about her motives. "I had Beth watching the store that day. She's a good worker, but we tend to get busy later in the day. Noon was the only time I could meet. Does that answer your question?"

She saw her friend's annoyance and rushed to explain. "He's only being thorough. Someone is still after me. Until we find out who, we have to question everyone and everything."

Trey placed his hands on Robin's shoulders. "It's fine," he said. "They're only asking questions, honey."

"Well, it doesn't feel like only asking questions. It feels like I'm being accused of something. Everyone is just so busy these days. I wanted to catch up with Melinda. That's all."

"I'm sorry," Melinda told her. "I'm glad we got together."

"Where were you on Saturday, Trey?" Noah asked.

He stiffened at the question. "I was purchasing supplies for the bakery. I work during the week, and it's the only day I can do the shopping. Some of the ingredients come in large bags that Robin can't lift."

That made sense to Melinda. In fact, everything they'd said seemed to add up. But Noah wasn't finished.

He took out his phone and pulled up the sketch of the attacker. "Do either of you know this man?"

Trey took the phone and studied the picture, then shook his head. "No, I don't know him."

He handed the phone to Robin, who glanced at it then twisted at the chain around her neck. "I've never seen that man before."

"Are you sure?"

Trey pushed the phone back to him. "We don't know him. Are we done? Because Robin and I have a business to run."

Melinda grimaced at his brisk tone. It seemed he'd changed his mind about the questioning. She hated alienating her friends, but they had to understand her predicament. Thankfully, Noah was done asking questions.

He nodded then reached for Trey's hand. "Thanks for understanding. I was only trying to do what's best for Melinda."

Melinda retrieved Ramey, who had finished his cupcake and started on a cookie. They headed for the front of the store to leave, but she turned to Robin one last time before stepping outside. "I did enjoy our lunch together. We should do it again soon, okay?"

"Absolutely," Robin said, but Melinda noticed her enthusiasm didn't match her words as she quickly retreated into the kitchen. That upset her. Robin had been one of the first women to befriend her when she arrived in town.

Melinda bent down to help Ramey with his coat, and as she did, something shattered the window and buzzed past her, slamming into the plastic menu above the counter.

"Gun!" Noah shouted, grabbing Melinda and pulling her to the floor before she could straighten up. Bending down to help her son had just saved her life. "Get down!"

Ramey cried out at the commotion, and Noah saw fear on Melinda's face. Two other customers in the bakery—and Beth behind the counter—had also hit the floor when the shots started. He stared at them now, huddled and frightened.

"Is everyone okay?" Robin called, then screamed and ran back into the kitchen as another shot was fired through the front window.

Noah pulled Melinda and Ramey beneath a table, then drew his gun and crawled to the window. It was immediately obvious there were too many people around for him to try to get off a return shot, even if he could figure out where the gunfire was coming from. His handgun didn't have the accuracy of a rifle, and it was too great a risk of hitting someone besides his target. He had more powerful weapons in the trunk of his car, but he doubted he could get to them before this was all over.

He tried to get a look at the shooter. He saw nothing for several moments, then another shot rang out and he saw where the gunfire was coming from. "He's firing from across the street. Top of the building."

"That's Mona Milburn's boutique," Melinda told him.

"He probably crawled up the back of the building." He pulled out his phone and dialed 911. "There's a sniper on the roof of Mona Millburn's shop. He's shooting into the Danbars' bakery."

The operator promised to relay the message and dispatch units to the scene. At least the gunfire had scattered the crowds on the street, clearing the way for the police to approach.

"What should we do?" Melinda asked.

He turned to look at her. Fear was lining her face as she hugged Ramey to her. He hated seeing that look of despair on her face. "Try to make it to the kitchen, but stay low." He glanced at the others and told them the same thing. "Stay low so he can't see you."

They all started crawling on the floor, Melinda pulling Ramey beside her while simultaneously pushing his head low. Once they reached the kitchen, she leaped to her feet and dragged Ramey along with her toward the back of the building.

Noah followed their lead and crawled across the floor to the kitchen, which was windowless and blocked off by a large wall between the front area and the kitchen.

He stood and dusted off. "Is everyone okay?" He counted heads as they all nodded and remarked they were unhurt. Melinda and Ramey were there, as were Robin and Beth and the two customers who'd been in the bakery when the shooting started. But someone was missing. "Where's Trey?"

Robin looked frazzled as Noah turned his attention toward her. "He left right after you two walked out." She pulled at the chain around her neck holding a delicate cross. He'd noticed her playing with it before, when she'd seen the sketch, and suspected she was hiding something then. Now he knew she was.

"Where did he go?"

"I—I don't know. He was furious at the questions you were asking and said he needed time to cool off."

The sound of sirens approaching was the only thing that prevented Noah from calling her out. It was much too coincidental that her husband had disappeared at exactly the moment someone had started shooting at them. And who else had known they were inside the bakery?

His phone buzzed and he answered it. It was Peterson.

"Is everyone okay in there?"

"We're all fine. No one was hit. What's the status?"

"Whoever it was is gone. I've got teams spreading out and forming a perimeter."

He glanced at Robin then turned around. "I have someone you can keep an eye out for. Trey Danbar."

"Trey? Why?"

"He's MIA from the bakery, but he was here just

before the shooting started. I'm not sure he had time to get out and get on top of the building, but something is definitely weird with him."

"Will do," Peterson stated. "For now, stay put inside until we've completed our sweep of the area."

He disconnected the call and slipped his phone back into his pocket. His heart was starting to slow, but it broke to see Melinda and Ramey huddled together in fear. It had been a bad call to bring her out in the open, and he kicked himself for thinking he could keep her safe. He had to do better.

His instinct was to pull her into his arms and comfort her, but each error in judgment he had made was because of his selfish desire to keep her by his side. He had to think smarter, and he couldn't allow his feelings for this lady to cloud his rational thinking. There may be no future for them together, but he was determined to make certain she at least *had* a future.

Melinda rolled up her jacket and used it as a pillow for Ramey to lie on. It was way past his bedtime, and even with the noise of the police station, he was out like a light in a matter of minutes. She draped Noah's jacket over him, then went to find out what was going on. All her energies for the past hour had been spent keeping her son calm. Now that he was asleep and they were safe at the station, she could truly focus on what was happening with the investigation.

Trey Danbar had tried to shoot her.

She couldn't wrap her brain around it. Why would

Trey want to harm her? She found Noah and Chief Peterson talking and interrupted their conversation.

"How's Ramey?" Noah asked, and she loved that his first thought was of her son.

"He's fine. What's happening?"

"We found Trey and swabbed his hands," Peterson said. "There was no evidence of gunpowder, meaning he wasn't the shooter."

Noah frowned. "Then where was he?"

"He said he headed home, just like Robin said."

Noah shook his head. "No way he left that fast unless he had somewhere pressing to be."

"My officers found no weapons on him, but they did find he made a call minutes before the shooting started."

Noah turned to her. "Robin went into the office to get Trey. He could have made a phone call before he came out, alerting whoever would be shooting at us that we were there."

"Or anyone could have known because they saw us walk in. The streets were crowded with people."

Noah shook his head. "No, it would have taken too long for him to set up. He wouldn't have any idea how long we would be inside. We could have come in and walked right back out."

"He was on top of a building. He could have shot at us anywhere on the street." All the back and forth and speculation was exhausting. "What about the number Trey called? Who did it belong to?"

Chief Peterson shook his head. "I had my guys run it, but it came back as a burner phone."

"I don't understand why Trey would want to hurt me. Robin and I have been friends for years."

"Well, we've got both Trey and Robin detained separately. We'll find out what's going on." He glanced at Melinda. "Do you mind if Noah and I speak privately for a moment?"

She was curious what all the secrecy was about, then decided she didn't really want to know. She had enough on her mind and was sure Noah would fill her in on whatever they were talking about. "Sure. I'll go get a cup of coffee."

She watched them enter Chief Peterson's office, where he handed Noah a file. She could guess what was in it. He was looking into Sean's death. She supposed it had to be done, but she wanted no part of those memories. Seeing his cold, dark eyes had been enough to convince her he was alive.

She walked into the small break room. Someone had made a fresh pot of coffee, and she helped herself to a cup. She was ready for this night to be over. Ramey needed to be in a bed, and she had to admit she was tired enough to crash herself.

She turned and started, dropping her coffee as she spotted Wayne Lassiter blocking the doorway and trapping her inside the break room.

Although she was fairly certain he wasn't involved in the threats against her life, she still suspected he'd had a hand in Nikki's disappearance. Either way, she wanted nothing to do with him.

"What are you doing here, Wayne? I thought the police were questioning you."

"They had to let me go. I haven't done anything. Someone stole my car and used it to attack you, Melinda. I'm completely innocent."

His blameless expression made her furious. "There is nothing innocent about you, Wayne."

"Are you still harping on the Nikki thing?"

"You mean her disappearance and probable murder? Yes, I am."

"I had nothing to do with that, either. I wish someone would find her and bring her home."

She wanted to tell him about the blood evidence that had been found in his car, but she didn't know what the investigators who'd questioned him had told him, and she didn't want to jeopardize the case by making him aware of physical evidence against him if he didn't already know. But she could not wait for the day that that smug grin was wiped from his face when she filed a murder indictment against him.

"Why are you here, Wayne? I mean, what compelled you to stop and talk to me? We're not friends."

"No, we're not. Never have been. I know you've never liked me, but there's something you should know about Noah Cason, and since you're a former friend of my wife's, I felt like it was my duty to tell you about it."

She didn't miss the *former friend* part. Past tense. "I know everything I need to know about him."

He shook his finger at her in a condescending manner. "You're too trusting, just as Nikki was. You have no idea what kind of man you've associated yourself with."

"What are you talking about?"

"Nikki thought he was a hero, but that wasn't true. He's a killer, Melinda."

She stared into his eyes, stunned by the irony of what he was saying. Who was Wayne Lassiter to call Noah a killer? "You know nothing. If he's killed, it was in the line of duty."

"No, he was a killer before he even joined the navy. He murdered his and Nikki's father when he was sixteen."

She gasped at the accusation. This man would go to any lengths to paint himself as the good guy.

"Did he forget to tell you? Nikki told me all about it years ago. Lyle showed me the police report. Their mother came home to find her husband dead and Noah holding the bloody knife. His mother even testified against him at trial."

Melinda was stunned. Why would Wayne go to the trouble of telling her a lie he knew she could disprove by looking into it? "There was a trial?"

"He apparently got off on a technicality and joined the navy soon afterward. You can look it up if you don't believe me. It took place in Monroe County. You'll see I'm right. You're hanging around with a killer, Melinda. You're pinning all your hopes and dreams on a murderer."

He turned and walked away, but his words left her reeling. Nikki had never had anything but good things to say about her brother, but then again, she'd had nothing but good words for her husband, too, until Melinda had confronted her about the abuse. But why did Wayne care about her knowing this? Was it just to hurt her? That was the most likely scenario. Perhaps he thought by distracting her, she would give up on pinning Nikki's disappearance on him.

She was cleaning up the spilled coffee when another figure appeared in the doorway. She glanced up to see Noah standing over her.

"What happened?" he asked.

"I had a little accident." She tossed the wet paper towels into the trash. "What's going on? What was all that about?"

"He wanted to give me some information about your husband. That, and he wanted to tell me they had to let Wayne go."

She folded her arms protectively against her chest, hating the doubt that Wayne had planted. She was sure that had been his sole intention. "I know. I saw him."

"You did?" He stepped closer to her and touched her shoulder. "He didn't hurt you, did he?" He meant the gesture to be comforting, but to Melinda, his hand on her felt like a boulder she couldn't shove off.

"No, he didn't hurt me." But he had. He'd devastated her without ever laying a finger on her.

"Good. Why don't we go? It's past time for Ramey to be in bed."

"Sure, but I need to talk to Chief Peterson privately for a moment, too. Can you wait?"

"No problem. You want me to go ahead and load Ramey into the car?"

"I'll only be a minute." She marched past him and into Peterson's office, closing the door behind her.

He looked up from his desk. "If this is about what Noah and I—"

"This has nothing to do with that. How could you not tell me about Noah's past? Your friend Wayne couldn't wait to stop me in the break room and spill the beans. He said you knew Noah was arrested for killing his father?"

"That was years ago, Melinda."

"Is that supposed to make me feel better? Have I allowed a dangerous man into my life? Around my son?"

"Wayne told me about Noah after Nikki vanished. He wanted me to look into her brother as a possible suspect."

"He wasn't even in the country when she vanished."

"I know. That's what I discovered when I checked into him. But I had to look. Wayne suggested he was violent, and even told me about the incident Nikki had told him about. He claimed Nikki was scared of him, and the last time she'd spoken to him, he'd told her he was coming to town."

She shook her head at the absurdity of Wayne's attempts to distract from his own actions. "You don't really believe he was involved in Nikki's disappearance, do you?"

"No, I don't. I called his lawyer, a public defender at the time. He told me the real story. Apparently, their father was abusive to them both growing up. When Noah was sixteen, he found him beating up Nikki. He tried to stop him and wound up stabbing him to get him to stop. Nikki was almost killed that night. He saved her life. She testified to the abuse at his trial, and he was acquitted."

"He was protecting her?" She glanced out the office window and saw Noah sitting protectively beside Ramey. She suddenly felt like a gigantic fool. "Wayne was trying to make me doubt him."

"I've been a police officer for sixteen years. During that time, I've had to pull my gun on multiple occasions, but I've only shot it three times. One of those three was fatal. It was a good shot, but it still haunts me to know I took someone's life. I imagine Noah's had to make that choice many times throughout his career, but I can't imagine you become immune to it. Talk to him. You may be the only person who's ever wanted to listen to his side of that terrible night."

It was good advice, and she appreciated it. Her fear and anger was dissipating at his reassurances. She thanked him, then walked back to the waiting area to tell Noah she was ready to leave. He picked up Ramey and carried him to the car, and she was struck by his gentleness with him. She wanted to believe Noah was a good person and wouldn't have hurt anyone without provocation, and she hadn't, until Wayne had placed doubts in her mind.

But why had he never told her about this? Was he afraid of what she might think? She'd told him her deepest, darkest secret about killing her husband, and he'd said nothing to her in return about this. She was already wary about putting her heart out there, and she'd sworn she would never again fall for an abusive man.

Was it possible Noah had fooled her the same way Sean had?

And was it already too late for her to guard her heart against him?

Noah waited until Melinda tucked Ramey into bed, then disappeared into the bedroom herself before he opened the file on Sean Steele. Noah stared at the photographs of Melinda in the case file, beaten and bruised. He felt sick. And angry. And disgusted.

He'd known about the abuse, but knowing it and seeing it were two different things. If Sean wasn't really dead, Noah couldn't wait to get his hands on him and make him pay for how he'd treated Melinda.

He read through the police report that documented Melinda's tale of being taken out on a boat on the lake by her husband, then being thrown overboard and held under the water. The report was full of facts and reports, but few conclusions. Sean Steele was officially listed as missing, and the case was still technically open.

She'd told him Sean had been declared legally deceased six months ago. That meant someone had checked to make certain his social security number hadn't been used and his credit reports had been inactive for all that time. If he was alive and targeting Melinda, how was he surviving?

There were ways of living off the grid, but why would Sean take that route if he didn't have to? Had something else happened on that boat that Melinda hadn't told him about? Something that would make him run? Given their history, Noah had a difficult time believing Sean would be worried about the attack on Melinda. He'd talked and threatened his way out of other violent incidents. There was no reason to suspect he couldn't have this time, as well.

He pulled a photograph of Sean Steele from the file. It was his mug shot, taken during one of his domestic violence arrests. He pulled up the image of the sketch he'd helped create and compared the two.

The similarities were there, enough that he could understand why Melinda would think this man was her husband. But this mug shot was ten years old. It might be him, but Noah couldn't tell for certain.

Noah pushed away the file and rubbed his face. This was all starting to get to him, but protecting Melinda was his number-one priority. He knew Nikki wouldn't mind. She would want him to take care of Melinda, especially when the odds of finding her alive were negligible.

He opened his laptop and pulled up a map of the Southeast, calculating the distance between Daytonville and Lakewater, Tennessee, where Melinda had lived when Sean died. It was only a three-hour drive. He could go there and be back in a day, albeit a long one. He wanted to talk to the local sheriff's office and get the real dish on what had happened and what kind of man Sean Steele had been. He knew from experience that not everything went into logs and reports.

Melinda wouldn't like it. And he wouldn't like leaving her alone, but he would make certain she was protected while he was gone. Peterson had proven himself trustworthy in Noah's eyes, and he felt sure he would watch over her for one day.

He was so caught up in making his plans that he didn't even see Melinda had entered the room.

She stared at the file he'd left open on the table with an image of her battered face, clear as day. "It's awful, isn't it?"

"Yes, it is."

"I know you could never want someone like me." Her voice had a hint of sorrow to it that angered him.

"Do you think I blame you for what happened with your husband? I'm proud of you for standing up to him, for fighting back."

"I should have done it sooner. Maybe then he would be alive."

"Or maybe he would have killed you. You did what you had to do, Melinda, and you survived. That's an amazing thing. It's not something to feel guilty about."

"Is that how you feel about what you did?"

For a moment he was confused. Was she talking about the embassy and the people he'd let die? Or letting down Nikki?

She must have seen the confused look on his face because she clarified. "I'm talking about what happened with your father."

That caught him off guard and nearly knocked the breath from him. "So you know about that?" Had Nikki confided in her and she'd waited this long, only to throw that incident in his face?

She looked down as she revealed the source of her information. "Wayne mentioned it to me."

Noah turned away from her. That blow was difficult to take.

"He was at the police station. I think he was trying to make himself look better by tearing you down."

"I see it worked."

"No, Noah, it didn't. I know it was justified and you were acquitted. I only want to know if that makes it feel better, because I've been sick to my stomach since the day that happened with Sean. No matter what he did to me, he didn't deserve to die. I took his life. I took him away from his child."

"A child he didn't even want, Melinda. A child he was trying to murder."

She took in a deep breath to try to slow down the fiery pace they were heading toward. "All I'm saying is it changed me. I wonder if it changed you, as well?"

How did he even answer that? Of course it had changed him. He'd done his duty to protect his sister, but only after they'd both suffered years of abuse. He hadn't acted swiftly enough then, and he hadn't acted swiftly enough at the embassy. People died because of it, his father included. "I did what I had to do," he told her. "So did you. That's the only thing that matters."

He closed the file and his laptop. "I need to make a trip tomorrow. I want to go to Lakewater."

"Why? You have the report. You know what happened."

"There are always things that aren't in the report. Look, Melinda, I don't believe this is Sean, but we need to put this question to rest, not only so we can find the person who has targeted you, but so that you can finally have peace about it, too. I can see how this has been weighing on you all these years. I want to finally put this behind you."

He touched her beautiful, delicate face, and his heart broke at all she'd been through.

"I'm afraid," she finally confessed, her brown eyes staring up into his.

He longed to pull her into his arms and reassure her, but what she'd said about Wayne troubled him. Had he managed to plant doubts in her mind about him? Had her opinion changed? It seemed to him she could see right through him to his fears and insecurities. "I know how frightening it can be to face your past. But if you're not ready, then I understand. I still need to go. Will that be okay?"

"I understand why you think you have to go," she told him, "but I can't go back there. I won't."

"I'll just be gone one day. I'll drop you off at the police station after we take Ramey to school, then I'll be back by the afternoon."

"I don't like it, but I won't stop you. I hope you're not disappointed at what you find." She padded across the floor and disappeared back into the bedroom.

He got up and stared out at the lake in the distance, and his mind turned to God. He wished he had more faith that God would watch over her and keep her safe, but he'd lost his trust in God months ago. Terrible things kept happening, and the God he'd trusted for most of his life allowed it.

Yet he couldn't deny that in his most frantic state, when he'd thought Melinda had drowned, he'd called out to God for help and, that time at least, He'd come through. Melinda had been okay.

But Nikki hadn't been okay.

And neither had his teammates.

Evil and chaos had reigned that night three months ago in Libya, and he could still hear the screams of rage and the cries for help. He still tasted the smoke and soot that had filled his lungs as he crawled through the embassy to find survivors.

He hadn't even had the opportunity to tell Melinda about his time in Libya or what he really did for a living now. But his covert security training didn't seem to be making much difference in keeping her safe now.

Noah sank down into the cushions of the sofa. If God wanted to help him out by watching over Melinda and Ramey a little closer tomorrow, that would be fine by him. Because tomorrow morning he was headed to Lakewater, Tennessee, and he was going to find out the truth about Sean Steele's death.

SEVEN

Lakewater, Tennessee, turned out to be everything Noah had expected it to be. It was smaller than Daytonville and even smaller than the place he and Nikki had grown up. The town had two stoplights on Main Street, and most of its shops were boarded up and covered with graffiti.

He found the sheriff's office and parked the car, bracing himself for what he was about to learn. In all likelihood it wouldn't be pleasant, but he had to do this if he wanted to put the question of Sean Steele to rest.

He got out of the car and walked inside. He told the desk clerk what he was looking for, and was greeted a few minutes later by a deputy with a name tag that read Walters. Noah stood, shook his hand and introduced himself.

"You're here about the Steele case? I faxed a copy of that file over to Chief Peterson of the Daytonville Alabama Police Department. Are you one of them?"

"Not quite. Chief Peterson did show me the file, but I had some more questions about the case. I was hoping by coming here I could clear up some things."

"What's your concern in this matter, Mr. Cason?"

"Well, I'm a friend of Melinda Steele. I'm acting on her behalf. There may be a chance Sean is alive."

Deputy Walters shook his head. "Not likely." He waved Noah back through the bullpen and into what looked like an evidence room. "We had some clothes wash up a few years ago. There was no one around to identify it, but we're all pretty sure it belonged to Sean." He dug through a box and produced a plastic bag with pieces of clothing inside.

"That wasn't in the report you faxed over."

"It's not part of that file, since it's never been officially identified."

"Why do you think it belonged to him?"

"There's stitching on this piece that looks like an *S*. Sean always had initials stitched into his shirts. It was one of those things everyone knew about him. I think he thought it made him look cool or something."

"You knew Sean and Melinda?"

"Sure, I knew them. We all grew up together."

"So you knew about the abuse she suffered? Yet he was never arrested on domestic violence charges?"

"Everyone knew how Sean was, but there was never enough evidence to convict him. The women, Melinda included, always recanted."

Noah sighed. He was tired of hearing that phrase. Not enough evidence. Not enough to implicate Wayne in Nikki's disappearance. Not enough to authorize a rescue plan on the embassy.

"And the day he died. Tell me what happened."

"You've read the report. Sean and Melinda went

out on the boat. Only Melinda came back. She claimed he'd tried to drown her and went overboard. It was clear she'd taken a beating. We searched the lake but never found his body. We did find blood on the boat that turned out to be his."

"And you've never had any reason to suspect he didn't die that day?"

Deputy Walters shook his head. "None."

"I'd like to see where it happened," Noah said. "Will you take me out there?"

Noah rode with Deputy Walters out to a spot on the lake and climbed out of the car.

"Of course, you can't see the exact spot from here," Walters said, "but they were docked out that way. There are a lot of rock formations in this lake. I suspect he either hit his head when he fell or hit one of those rocks and blood splattered. Either way, he never resurfaced."

The lake was murky, and seeing to the bottom was impossible. He imagined the moment, Sean bringing her out here and holding her down, trying to drown her, and Melinda fighting back. He'd seen her spunk and determination. Her fight to live must have surprised him. He liked that.

"What about her family?" he asked the deputy. "What did they think about her story?"

"What family? Melinda had no family. She was raised by her grandmother, who died when she was sixteen. She was already dating Sean so she moved in with the Steele family, and a few years later she married him."

That saddened him to hear. She'd had no one to look

out for her as a kid except for an aging grandmother. At least he and Nikki had had one another.

"How well did you know them?"

He shrugged. "It's a small town. Like I said, we all went to school together. Everyone knows everyone else's business."

"What about Sean's family? How did they react?"

"Oh well, they were outraged, as you can imagine. It was only his mom and younger brother still living here. The youngest kid, Tyler, moved out of state five years ago, not long after his mother passed away. Sean's older brother, Ray, is serving time upstate."

"On what charge?"

"Gun trafficking. He was caught up in a bust fifteen years ago by ATF. It was big news around here. He's serving thirty years. There were a few cousins, but they've mostly moved on with their lives."

"Any who might want to take revenge on Melinda?"

"After all this time? Doubtful. They were pretty riled up at the time, but once Melinda left town, it eventually all blew over. Sean's mom died two years after Melinda left town, and like I said, his younger brother, Tyler, left town soon after."

"Any idea where Tyler is now?"

"Atlanta, last I heard. No one around here has heard from him in years."

Noah shook Deputy Walters's hand. "Thank you for your time," he told him. "I think I've seen enough."

He walked back to his car and headed back toward Daytonville. No wonder she had run from this place. He wished she'd gotten out sooner, and never gotten involved with Sean Steele in the first place. This was the kind of life any of them could have gotten caught up in. If he hadn't joined the navy and learned discipline and routine, he might have become like Sean or like his father, violent and mean. Melinda had managed to get away from that life, too, but she'd paid a big price for her escape.

Was it possible Sean had somehow survived that day? It didn't make sense. Had he been alive, he would have taken his revenge a long time ago. And Noah couldn't imagine he would have missed his own mother's funeral.

No, Sean Steele was dead and gone. He was even more sure of it than before he'd come.

But it wouldn't hurt to look into Tyler. It was possible Sean's brother could look enough like him to pass for him in a sketch, and no one around here knew his whereabouts.

Noah turned on the windshield wipers as freezing rain began to fall. It was unusual weather for Alabama, but it had been an especially cold season so far. He was sixty miles from home…or at least what he was considering home for now. It amazed him how easily that image of home morphed into an image of Melinda wrapped in his arms.

He flipped on the radio, but the only station he could get reception on was a talk radio station, and the big news on that channel was the embassy attack and the ensuing drama of the contractors who'd been left out in the cold. For the first time in weeks, that hadn't been the thing weighing down his mind. In fact, now all that drama seemed a lifetime away. Keeping Melinda and Ramey safe was his only concern now.

Yet he couldn't let the events from that night go. He'd been foolish, pushing for his team to wait on official approval. He'd been so used to following rules and procedures that he'd allowed his hesitancy to cost lives.

He flipped off the radio. His life was spiraling out of control, and he didn't know how to stop it. He was worried about keeping Melinda safe, and even more worried about guarding his heart against her. He'd already let Nikki down, and he couldn't undo that. He'd never met any woman like Melinda. Her strength and determination for her son was admirable. He loved the way she fought for her son and did everything she could to make sure he knew he was loved. It was such a difference from the way he'd been raised. What would his life have been like if his mother had been as kind and gentle as Melinda? He couldn't even imagine it.

He didn't often think about settling down and starting a family. When he did, his usual response was just to push it out of his mind. He'd always believed he wasn't the type of person who got the wife and family. It was no secret why. He was afraid. He'd always been concerned about turning into his father. He'd grown up in violence, and his job now was all about violence. But he was good at what he did, and that frightened him even more. He never wanted to hurt a family the way his father had hurt theirs. He wouldn't be responsible for creating another messed-up person like himself.

But maybe, with someone like Melinda on his side, things would be different.

It was a surprising thought, and he didn't dismiss it as quickly as he should have. That hesitation, those few moments of thinking about it, planted a seed in his mind that he couldn't get rid of.

Was it possible?

He rubbed his face.

It used to be so much easier to push away those urges. He told himself lies that he was always meant to stay single and live the bachelor life. Yet he had never before come across a woman he wanted to make those things happen with. Melinda had changed all that.

He wanted her. He wanted to build a life with her and raise children with her. Yet even as he dreamed about having those things, he also knew she'd be smart to run the other way. He would never make a good husband or father. Thinking of it was too tempting. He wouldn't even daydream about it anymore.

He had to find a way to keep himself from falling hard for the beautiful brunette—like focusing on finding the person terrorizing her. Someone had a real serious hatred for her, and he couldn't imagine why. What could a widowed single mother have done to anyone to elicit such rage? But she was so much more than that. She was also a prosecuting attorney who'd incarcerated many people, although Peterson had said those leads had gone cold.

She'd also taken the time to befriend a woman like Nikki, someone she'd seen was in the same boat she'd been in, and tried to convince her to leave her abusive situation.

He sighed thinking about Nikki. She must have felt so trapped. He knew he did. He'd been trapped in that tunnel of violence ever since he could remember. He could play the dutiful soldier, following the rules and doing everything just and right. The news media were calling him and his friends heroes, but he felt nothing like one. Even on his best days, he couldn't get free of that tight grip his past still had on him. And it seemed like Melinda couldn't get rid of the grip her past had on her.

Together, they made quite a pair.

An hour later he pulled up at the house. Peterson was sitting in his car in the driveway, ready to be relieved. Noah had messaged him a half hour ago from a gas station that he was nearly there.

"Everything okay today?" he asked.

"A-okay," Peterson responded. "But I'm glad you're back. This being on alert all day is exhausting."

"Tell me about it," Noah stated.

"How did your mission go?"

"Good. I'm convinced it's not him, but he has a brother we might want to check into."

"Great. We'll do that tomorrow," Peterson said before starting up his car and driving off.

"See you then," Noah called.

He walked into the house and saw the light still on in the den and a roaring fire in the fireplace. Melinda was curled up on the couch with papers spread around her, but she was asleep. He reached for a blanket behind her to cover her with, but she jumped, suddenly awake.

"You frightened me," she said, then laughed. "I didn't mean to fall asleep. I was trying to wait up for you."

"You didn't have to do that."

She smiled at him. "I wanted to see you and find out how it went. Did you find what you were looking for?"

He stared at the fire then turned back to her. "I don't believe Sean is alive, Melinda. Whoever this is after you, it's not him."

She leaned back against the couch and studied him. "I'm not sure I believe that yet. He was so familiar."

"There may be a reason for that. Did you ever meet his brother Tyler?"

"Sure, I knew Tyler."

"Is it possible it was him attacking you?"

Melinda laughed. "No, it wasn't Tyler. Sean was big and broad. Tyler was always…well, Sean used to call him the runt of the litter. He was shorter and slimmer."

"A lot can change in seven years. He might have put on weight, grown a few inches."

"I don't think it was Tyler, not the boy I remember anyway."

"I'll check up on him regardless and find out what he's up to." He got up and knelt beside the fire, stoking it until it roared.

"I still wish I had left Sean sooner. Maybe then, this wouldn't be happening."

"We all have regrets, things we wish we'd done or not done." He had a million of them, from not acting sooner to stop his father's abuse to not preventing the deaths at the embassy. "I've seen and done terrible things, Melinda. It comes with the job."

"Being a Navy SEAL?"

He shook his head and joined her on the couch. "I left the SEALs two years ago. It was supposed to be about rescuing people and taking out the bad guys, but it seemed there was always another bad guy on the horizon. They're like weeds. You get rid of one, and six more grow. I guess I got disillusioned. It seemed the job turned more into taking out the enemy than rescuing.

"I've been working for an organization called the Security Operations Abroad, the SOA. We do contract security for the CIA. My last station was in Libya. My team responded to an attack on the embassy there a few months ago. You probably heard about it on the news."

She nodded. "I did. That was you?"

"Yes. We weren't supposed to go. We never got an official okay from the higher-ups, but we couldn't just wait around for people to die."

"Why wouldn't the government give you the okay to help?"

"They didn't want to jeopardize their secret CIA base. If we went in, someone would have to explain how we got there and why. We didn't care about all that politics. We heard the calls for help from the embassy and wanted to go."

She smiled up at him. "You're a hero."

"No, I'm not. When the call came, I hesitated. I wanted to wait for official word. It never came, and finally my team convinced me we couldn't wait any longer. I put my trust in my government to do the right thing. They failed me, just as I failed my team. I should have listened to them and not convinced them to wait. Because of my hesitation, two men in my team died, along with some from the embassy. Don't you see, Melinda? I failed my team. I failed Nikki. Now I'm failing to keep you and Ramey safe."

"You haven't failed me and Ramey. I'm still here because of you. And Nikki's disappearance wasn't your fault."

"I should have been here to protect her."

"I'm not sure it would have made a difference, Noah. She was stubborn, and she'd made up her mind to stay with Wayne." She reached for his hand and held it. "I'm sorry for what you went through at the embassy. I can't imagine all the things you've seen. God never planned for all this death and killing. It wasn't the life He wanted for us."

"He hasn't done much to prevent it."

"Of course He has. He's sent people like you to do battle."

He shook his head. "I don't fight for God, Melinda. I'm not even sure I believe in Him anymore."

"It doesn't matter if you believe in Him. I don't claim to have all the answers, Noah, but I have faith. I know God's character, and it's good and holy. If He allows us to hit rock bottom, maybe it's to show us that He is The Rock at the bottom."

He looked at her, in awe of her conviction. "How can you have such faith, Melinda? Look at all you've been through. How can you still believe that God is on your side?"

She gave him a small smile then squeezed his hand. "I'll admit I've been very disillusioned recently. Then I realized something. God hasn't abandoned me, Noah. He's been fighting for me. He sent me you to protect me and Ramey. He sent me a warrior."

"I'm no one's warrior. It seems lately I can't protect anyone. Nikki. My teammates. I can't save anyone, Melinda, and if I'm honest, I'm terrified of letting you and Ramey down. I'm worried I'm not enough to keep you safe."

She leaned over and placed a kiss on his cheek. "I believe in you, Noah. I believe in you."

She got up and went into the bedroom, closing the door behind her. He sat, the fire roaring and the room dark, staring into the flames. Part of him was thrilled Melinda believed in him. It gave him the affirmation he needed. But that tinge of doubt lingered. Was he good enough to keep them safe? And what would happen if he wasn't?

The next morning, after dropping Ramey off at school, Noah took Melinda to the library where her makeshift office had been set up, then he headed for the police station. He wanted to talk to Peterson about what he'd found in Lakewater.

"Sean has two brothers, Tyler and Ray. Ray's been in prison for years, but Tyler lives in Atlanta."

"So you're thinking it's Sean's brother who is responsible for these attacks against Melinda?"

"It makes more sense than her dead husband, doesn't it? The sheriff's deputy in Lakewater is sure he drowned that day, despite the fact that they never found his body. Besides, if he was alive, I feel certain he would have come looking for Melinda a long time ago."

Peterson nodded. "I'd have to agree." He sat down at his computer. "Okay, let's see what we have on Tyler Steele of Atlanta."

Noah walked behind him so he could see over his shoulder as Peterson pulled up the information.

"Looks like he's lived in Atlanta for four years. Works at a car dealership. No criminal charges or arrests on file." He pulled up his DMV file photograph. "And he looks nothing like his brother."

Noah examined the picture that popped up. Peterson was right. He looked nothing like Sean or even the man Noah had seen attacking him. Didn't seem likely that Tyler was involved. "What about the brother in prison... Ray?"

Peterson typed in some information, and Ray Steele's inmate photograph popped up. Noah's gut clenched. "That could be the guy who attacked us. How old is this photograph?"

"This was taken six years ago." Peterson leaned forward. "And look at this. He was paroled four months ago. He missed a meeting with his parole officer three months ago and hasn't been heard from since. If this is our guy, it makes sense. He hasn't been able to get to her all this time because he's been behind bars. Now that he's out, he wants revenge on her for killing his brother."

Noah agreed. "And he looks enough like Sean to freak her out and convince her that Sean isn't really dead." So it wasn't some ghost back from the dead. It was simple revenge for the death of his brother.

This news would shock her, but at least they had some answers now. And he knew who the bad guy was.

Noah picked up Melinda after lunch and drove her to her house to try to sort through the rubble. She nearly bawled at the sight of what was left of her home. Her Christmas lights were half hanging down, her lawn ornaments had been trampled and the water from the fire hoses had warped her floors.

She pushed through the door with Noah close behind her. The small Christmas tree she'd purchased and decorated so precisely was gone. Her photographs were burned, and all her furniture was ruined. She kicked through the rubble and searched for any photo, any shred of something she could salvage. She found very little.

The smell of smoke was everywhere, and she nearly gagged on it. She hurried back outside to the fresh air. Noah followed and pulled her into his arms.

The horror of the situation slammed into her. Sean was destroying her life piece by piece. "He did this, didn't he?" she asked, leaning into him. "Sean did this to me."

"No, he didn't," Noah insisted. "Sean is dead. Even

the police believe it. There's no reason to believe he's not."

"Then who is doing this to me?"

"This isn't exactly the place I wanted to have this conversation, but Sean had a brother."

She shook her head. "I told you. It wasn't Tyler." She could never mistake Tyler for Sean. They looked nothing alike.

"No, not Tyler. Ray."

"Ray? He's in prison."

"No, he was paroled four months ago. He has the same build as Sean. Same coloring and looks. And you said you'd never met him. It's possible you only thought it was Sean because of the similarities."

She gasped at the idea. She knew her own husband...didn't she? She'd never met Ray before, but she supposed it was possible he looked enough like his brother to fool her. It had, after all, been seven years since she'd seen Sean. "Ray? Are you sure?"

"It fits. I think he's been here, watching you, learning your routine. He knows you've gotten on with your life, and he's angry about losing his brother. This is his payback."

It was suddenly all too much. "I don't think I can do this," she told him.

"Yes, you can. And I'm right here beside you. We'll get through this together."

She stared up into his eyes. She could get lost in them, she knew.

Melinda soaked in the presence of him. She'd longed for someone like Noah for so long. Yet she'd pushed those desires back for years, focusing on Ramey and building a life for him, but she'd never forgotten her dreams of falling in love with someone good and kind.

To tell the truth, she'd never believed it would happen for her. She'd fallen hard for Sean, only to be disappointed and disillusioned with his kind of love. It had made her cynical and afraid to take another chance on love.

Finally, she went back inside and did her best to sort through the mess that was her house and her belongings.

It turned out that what she could salvage could be loaded into two boxes. Noah loaded them into the back seat of his car.

"That's it," she told him. "That's all that's left of my life."

He sighed. "Maybe, but you can always rebuild. What's important is that you're alive." He flashed her a mischievous smile. "I, for one, am extremely happy about that. I've grown to like you a little bit."

She liked his teasing tone. In fact, she liked everything about him, and he had become such an important part of her life in the past few days. Had it only been days since he'd first strolled into her office and demanded to know why Wayne wasn't in jail? It seemed like forever ago.

She didn't want to live her life on the periphery any longer. If all this had shown her anything, it was that she didn't want to be alone anymore. Yes, it was scary, but a good kind of scary. She didn't know if she was making a mistake, but something about Noah made it so easy for her to fall for him.

When he turned to her, she put her arms around his neck and leaned into him, pressing a soft kiss against his lips. She felt him tense, and his arms went around her, but then he pushed her away and stared into her eyes.

"I can't," he whispered. "I—I don't deserve this. I don't deserve you. I'm not a good person, Melinda."

She shook her head and touched his face. "You're a wonderful person, Noah. You're kind and brave and gentle. You've been there for me through all that's happened. You've protected me and my son. I can't even imagine what would have happened if you hadn't come here." She touched his face again, pulling it down to her lips. "You're my hero, Noah Cason," she said before their lips touched.

He didn't hold back this time, pressing into her and returning her kiss with all the love and passion inside him.

Her old life had ended, but perhaps it was time to take a chance on a new life with him.

They headed to the school to pick up Ramey, a new exciting spark now floating between them. She intertwined her fingers with his as he parked. She felt like a teenager again experiencing first love, and knew she couldn't wipe away the silly smile on her face even if she'd wanted to.

Children were already running toward their respective day-care vans and buses as she stepped onto the sidewalk and looked around for Ramey. He always met her by the pole at the front of the building, but she didn't see him anywhere. When the kids cleared out and Ramey still hadn't appeared, she grew concerned and asked one of the teachers on duty if they knew where he was.

She checked her clipboard. "It looks like he's already been picked up."

"Picked up? By who?"

"I don't have that information, but I see he's on the pick-up list. You can check with the office."

She glanced at Noah, trying not to let her panic show. The lightheartedness she'd felt earlier was gone. "Susan often picks up Ramey for me when I'm working a big case. Maybe we got our wires crossed today and she thought she was supposed to get him." She hurried into the office and glanced at the list. Sure enough, Susan had signed Ramey out of school several hours ago. But under the reason for early dismissal, she'd written "sick."

"Was he ill?" she asked the school secretary. "I didn't receive a call to come pick him up."

"I don't think anyone called. She just showed up to check him out." She seemed confused by Melinda's alarm. "Mrs. Campbell is on his list of authorized people who can sign him out."

"Yes, she is."

"Is there a problem?"

Melinda tried to hold it together, but inside she was screaming. She hadn't asked Susan to pick up Ramey today. And she certainly wouldn't have asked her to check him out early.

She walked out with Noah by her side, his arm reassuringly on her shoulder. "I'm sure there's a perfectly logical explanation," he told her, trying to help her remain calm and not let fear drive her crazy. "Maybe he got sick and his teacher couldn't reach you."

"That's not what the secretary said. She said no one called."

"She doesn't know everything. Call Susan. I'm sure this is all a misunderstanding."

He was right. She had to remain calm. If Susan picked up Ramey, then at least she knew he was safe. She took out her phone and dialed Susan's number, her hands shaking as she held the phone to her ear. It rang three times then went to voice mail. "She's not answering." Melinda tried again, hitting the redial button. Again, the call went to voice mail. She glanced at Noah and shook her head.

He opened the car door for her. "We'll go to her house."

She slid in and tried Susan's number again and again. She didn't pick up, which wasn't at all like her. Susan usually had her phone permanently attached to her hand. She was always on it, but for some reason today, the one day Melinda was counting on her being there, she wasn't.

Melinda immediately knew something was wrong when Noah pulled into Susan's driveway. Her garage door was up, but her SUV was gone. She got out and ran up to the house. The front door had been kicked in.

Her instinct was to rush inside screaming for her son, but Noah stepped in front of her and pulled his gun. He pushed open the door and looked around. Melinda followed him inside. Her first thought was that the house was too quiet. Two little boys made a lot of noise, but the house was eerily silent.

"Wait here," he told her as he moved through the house, clearing each room. He shook his head as he came back to her. "No one is here."

"Where could they be?" She was already fighting down hysteria, along with a thousand questions. Why would Susan pick up Ramey from school? And where had she taken him? And an even worse thought: Who had broken her front door in, and did it have anything to do with her actions?

Noah pulled out his phone. "I'll call Peterson and have him put a BOLO out for her car."

As Noah placed his call, Melinda walked into the playroom Susan had set up. Ramey loved spending time here, and Susan had always been so good to him. She didn't understand what was happening. Where was her son?

She picked up a stuffed rabbit she knew he liked to sleep with when he was here. She pressed it to her heart. *God, please let him be okay.*

She was so weary of running and being afraid, but this was much worse. This was a knife through her gut and a stab at the only thing she had left in the world.

Suddenly, a noise under the bed grabbed her attention. It sounded like a whimper. She dropped to her knees, her heart racing. Someone was hiding under the bed. Could it be Ramey? She leaned down and peeked under, spotting movement.

"Hello? Who's there?"

A small head popped up and a pair of big blue eyes peered at her. It was four-year-old Jason, not Ramey.

"Jason, honey, it's Melinda. Come on out. You're safe now."

He crawled out and went right into her arms. He was shaking and seemed so fragile.

"Jason, can you tell me what happened? Do you know where Ramey is?"

"He went with the man."

Melinda's heart stopped, and all the breath in her lungs seemed to vanish. "What man?" she managed to ask him. "Did you know this man?"

Jason shook his head. His eyes welled up and he started to cry. "He hurt my mommy."

"Where is your mommy?"

"Gone with the man. She told me to run and hide, so I did." He threw his arms around her neck and pressed himself against her. "I want my mommy," he said as he began to cry.

Noah must have heard him because he rushed into the room, his eyes wide with surprise.

She lifted Jason into her arms and did her best to comfort him. "He was hiding under the bed," she told Noah. "He said Ramey and Susan left with a man he didn't know."

"I'm afraid that's not really true," he told her. "I found her in the kitchen pantry."

She didn't need him to say the words, and she was

glad he didn't in front of Jason. She could tell by his expression that he hadn't found her alive.

She stroked Jason's hair and tried to comfort him, but inside she was sobbing. Her friend was dead, and her son was now in the hands of a killer.

EIGHT

Noah watched as Melinda sat huddled in the back seat of a police car. He hated seeing her this way, and he longed to hold her and reassure her that everything was going to be okay. He was going to bring Ramey home safely. But she didn't need his promises. She needed action.

Jason Campbell had been picked up by his grandmother and taken away, but not before being questioned. He hadn't been able to provide any further statements other than what he'd told Melinda. A man broke into his house and took his mother and Ramey away. But Noah knew there was more to it. Either he'd held Jason and threatened to kill him if Susan didn't go pick up Ramey from the school, or else she'd been in on it with him and then he'd double-crossed her. He hoped for Melinda's sake, it was the former. Her friend was dead and her son was missing. Nothing could worsen that feeling except maybe to discover that her friend had been complicit in her child's kidnapping.

Peterson approached him, but he didn't look like he

had good news. "We've canvassed the neighborhood, but so far no one saw anyone breaking into the house. Most people were at work when it happened."

"That makes sense. According to the school records, Susan picked Ramey up at ten forty-five this morning."

Peterson sighed. "That means he has about a six-hour head start."

"I don't think he's gone anywhere," Noah said. "Melinda has been his target all along. He probably took Ramey to get to her. He'll try to contact her."

"We didn't find a cell phone yet in the house. It's possible he has Susan's phone. I'm sure it has Melinda's cell phone number in it. I can have her number tracked. Maybe he has it on, and we can trace it."

"I doubt he'd be that dumb, but it's worth a try." Noah went back to their previous conversation from this afternoon. "Did you have a chance to call the warden at the prison where Ray Steele was housed?"

"I did, and the news isn't good. He said Ray Steele was a violent man. He was written up multiple times for brawling and assault, and only a few years ago he cleaned up his act. Became the model prisoner."

"After his brother died. He wanted to get out to avenge his death."

Peterson nodded. "And the parole board apparently bought it. The warden lobbied against him being released, but they didn't listen. He was released four months ago and hasn't been seen since."

Noah sighed. "Until now. So, he's been here in town watching her, learning all about her before he strikes?"

"It looks that way."

"How did he do that? How did he learn so much about her? He knew where she worked, where she lived, who her friends were, even how to get Ramey out of school. Someone had to be helping him."

Peterson glanced back at the house. "Susan Campbell, maybe?"

"Maybe."

"Why don't you take Melinda back to the safe house? She doesn't need to be here while we're processing the scene. Tell her to try to get some rest. We're doing everything we can to find Ramey."

Noah doubted it would do much good to try to reassure her, but he would do his best to keep her hopeful. If he was right, and Ray Steele had taken Ramey in order to get to her, that meant he wouldn't harm the boy…at least not until he got to Melinda.

He helped her to his car, hating the way she trembled in his arms. He wrapped his arm tighter around her shoulder.

She leaned her head against the headrest as he drove. Her hands shook. "He took him, didn't he? Ray took my son."

She turned her head away from him, but he heard her sobbing quietly. "I believe he'll try to make contact with you, Melinda. Peterson said he probably has Susan's phone. When he does, I need you to tell me. He'll probably try to lure you to him. You can't fall for that. You have to tell me. You have to trust me."

"Trust you?" She turned to him, anger in her expression and nails in her words. "How can I trust you? You promised me you would keep us safe and now Ramey is gone. He's in the hands of a killer."

Her words were like blows to his gut. He stopped the car in front of the safe house and reached for her arm.

She jerked away from him. "Don't touch me. Don't ever touch me again. I should have known better than to trust you, Noah. I let down my guard with you, but you're just like the Seans and Rays of the world. You're all alike and I can't trust any of you." She jumped from the car. He got out, too, calling her name, trying to get her to stop and talk to him.

She didn't stop. She hurried inside and ran to the bedroom, slamming and locking the door behind her.

He wanted to explain, but what could he say? She was right. He had failed her. He'd failed again, failed to protect this family he'd grown to love. He had no idea where Ramey was.

Grief washed over him. He leaned his head onto the door frame and just let it come. It didn't make any sense to him. *Why God? Why do You continue to allow this?*

He didn't understand how a good God could keep letting the bad guys win.

Melinda heard a soft knock on the bedroom door, then Noah's voice drifted through.

"Melinda? Chief Peterson is here. He wants to talk to us."

Panic burst through her, but she got up and went into the living room. The chief looked agitated as she entered. A frown covered his face, and his expression was forlorn. She'd only seen him this way on a handful of occasions, and none of them had resulted in good news.

"What is it?" she asked him. "Is it Ramey? Have you found him?"

"No, Melinda. It's nothing like that. We're still following up leads on Ramey's kidnapping, but we'll find him."

"What is it, then?" Noah asked him.

"It's about Wayne. As you know, his car was taken in as evidence in one of the attacks on you, Melinda. It keeps giving us possible links to Nikki."

"How?"

"As you know, Wayne travels a lot for his job. He has a GPS tracker in his car. It also happens to have a mileage tracker, which he uses for business."

"A lot of people have those nowadays."

"Yes, but we were looking through his to find out where the car had been. He's claimed in all his interviews that he was at home all night the day before Nikki went missing. His tracker tells a different story. There was an eighty-mile round trip taken the night before Nikki was reported missing."

Melinda gasped. "He used his own car. Unbelievable."

"The way I see it, he drove forty miles away, dumped her body, then drove home and went to bed. The next morning he acted like nothing had happened. I've got a team working on the search coordinates in all directions from forty miles out. We'll be getting new search parameters shortly." He glanced at Melinda. "Of course, I still have men searching for Ramey."

Noah shook his head. "You're stretching yourselves too thin. Ramey is the priority. If Nikki is buried out there somewhere, she's not going anywhere."

"I have officers tailing Wayne twenty-four-seven. If he tries to move her body, we'll catch him."

Noah thanked him and Peterson left.

As he walked up behind her, Melinda couldn't help but feel a connection to Nikki through him. They were very much alike in their mannerisms. "I miss her," she told him. "This is just the sort of thing I would call Nikki and talk to her about. And she always managed to make you feel better. No matter what she was going through, no matter how difficult her life was, she was always there with a smile on her face and a shoulder to cry on."

He smiled. "She was that way as a kid, too."

She turned to face Noah. "You didn't have to say that about Ramey being the priority. I know how badly you want to find your sister."

"And I will. I haven't given up on that, but Nikki's likely not going anywhere. There's still time to bring Ramey home."

She folded her arms and tried not to get angry. He meant well, but she couldn't push away the feeling that if he'd been here, if he hadn't gone chasing down Sean's memory, Ramey would still be with her.

He reached for her, but she pushed his hand away.

"I can't. I never should have trusted you. I'll never trust anyone else as long as I live."

She ran into the bedroom and fell onto the bed as sobs racked her again. She didn't mean to be so ugly toward Noah, but the last thing she wanted from him was to hear him tell her again how sorry he was.

She had to stop crying and trust that everything was going to be okay, but she couldn't. Fear had taken control, and she couldn't push away the horrible images of what might be happening to her child.

She'd never met Ray, but she remembered Sean talking about him and how dangerous he was. Now he was targeting her for something she'd done. Ramey was being punished because of her. That wasn't right. It wasn't the way it was supposed to be. It should have been her. It wasn't Ramey's fault that she'd killed Sean, but the worst way to hurt her was to harm her son.

Would his connection to Ramey, the fact that he was Ray's nephew, make any difference to Ray? He doubted it. He'd always believed Ray felt the same way Sean did—that family was his property, his possession. What would that mean for Ray? If he considered Melinda Sean's murderer, how would he view Ramey?

She could only pray it would be favorably.

Her phone buzzed. It was probably Noah checking on her again. She felt sorry for what she'd said to him. She'd been angry and hurt. She didn't really blame him. How could she? He was the one constant in her life now, and she needed him.

She glanced at the screen. It wasn't Noah. The message came from Susan Campbell's phone.

Meet me at the marina. Come alone or the kid dies.

She gasped. Ray! It had to be him.
Her fingers shook as she typed a response.

Is Ramey safe?

He's fine…for now. Come alone. You have a half hour then you'll never see the kid again.

Her motherly side was ready to bolt for the door, but somehow, she remembered Ray couldn't be trusted.

I want to talk to him.

No!

I don't go anywhere until I talk to him.

It hurt her heart to type those words, but she needed to know he was safe.

Her phone rang and she jumped, nearly dropping it. Susan's number popped up and she connected the call. Her knees buckled when she heard her son's voice.

"Mommy!"

"Ramey! Are you okay, baby?"

"I'm scared, Mommy." She thought her heart would burst at the fear she heard in his voice.

"I know, I know. I'm coming. I'm on my way."

It no longer mattered that she was walking into a trap. She had to go.

She quietly opened her bedroom door and looked around. She spotted Noah outside on the balcony, leaning against the rails. He looked so pitiful that she wanted to go to him, but she couldn't. Regardless of what he'd said to her in the car, she couldn't tell him about this. Ray had promised to kill Ramey if she didn't come alone, and the sting of distrust was just too strong. She couldn't put her son's life at risk again. Noah couldn't know about this phone call.

She spotted the car keys on the table and grabbed them, then snuck out the front door before Noah walked back inside. She ran to the car and hopped in. In her mind, she knew what she was doing wasn't smart, but that no longer mattered. She would do whatever it took to keep her child safe, even if that meant giving her own life to do it.

She started the car and took off for the marina.

Noah heard a car and rushed back inside to the front window. It was his own car pulling away!

He ran to Melinda's room, praying she was still there asleep on the bed. He pushed open the door. The bed was empty. She was gone.

But had she left on her own? Or had Ray Steele somehow gotten inside while he wasn't paying attention?

He pulled out his phone and called Peterson. "It's Melinda. She's gone."

"What? When? How?" He sounded as perplexed as Noah felt.

"Just now. Someone drove away in my car. I don't

know if she was alone or if Ray got her, but I need you here now."

"I'm on my way."

"Do you think he contacted her?"

Noah pinched the bridge of his nose as a feeling of helplessness overwhelmed him. "Probably." It seemed the most likely scenario. They'd been careful coming to and from the safe house. Ray must have phoned her from Susan Campbell's number and threatened to hurt Ramey if she didn't come.

And she hadn't trusted him enough to tell him so.

Peterson sighed. "I'll have someone put a BOLO out on your car and check her cell phone records."

Noah had nothing to do but wait, but he couldn't stay still, so he headed on foot down the hill. A thousand thoughts rushed through his mind as he hiked. Melinda didn't trust him, and she had good reason not to. He hadn't kept his word. He'd allowed both her and Ramey to get past him and into the hands of Ray Steele. Noah searched his brain for some clue as to what he may be up to. He'd taken everything from her—her home, her job, her son…everything but her life, and Noah feared that was next.

He thought back to the story he'd learned about Sean. If Ray was out to torture her, he would take her to the same place his brother had tried to dispose of her. It was also the thing that frightened her the most. But surely, he wouldn't take her all the way back to Lakewater to do the deed. No, he would find a comparable place close by.

A car approached him, and he instinctively reached

for his gun, relaxing when he saw it was Peterson. He hopped into the passenger's seat.

"Any idea where he would take her?" Peterson asked.

Noah couldn't even imagine where or what he might subject her to.

Somewhere near the water. But where?

"What about your rental car?" Peterson asked. "Does it have GPS?"

"It's a rental. I'll have to call the rental agency. Maybe they can give me the coordinates." He took out his phone and dialed the number for the rental agency.

"My name is Noah Cason," he said when a woman answered. "I rented a car from your agency several days ago. It's missing. I need you to give me the GPS coordinates."

"Sir, if the car has been stolen, then you'll need to file a police report."

"No, it hasn't been stolen. It's just been…misplaced. I just need those GPS coordinates."

"I'm sorry, I can't give you that information. We would need a police report. If you'd like to leave your name and number, I'll have someone call you back."

He left his information then disconnected the call, irritated by his lack of progress. "By the time they get back to me, it could be too late."

Peterson turned into downtown. "Okay, then we go back to the police station and check in on the BOLO, see if anything has been called in. If it hasn't, we go back through our suspects list. Despite my initial be-lief about Dawn, we haven't found anything to indicate either she or Susan had any prior connection with Ray Steele."

"Did Dawn or Susan have any properties that you're aware of where he might have gone?"

"I don't believe so. Dawn lived in an apartment, not very private, and Susan's house is still a crime scene. He wouldn't go there."

Peterson turned onto Main Street, passing the bakery Robin Danbar owned.

"What about Robin and Trey?" Noah asked. He still wasn't convinced they hadn't tipped off Ray about Melinda being in the bakery. If they had, it meant they were somehow involved with him.

Peterson glanced his way. "We never were able to trace who Trey made that call to."

"I want to talk to them again."

Peterson pulled over, and they got out of the car in front of the bakery. The sign said Open, but when he tried the door, it was locked. Noah saw a light on in the back and knocked on the glass.

"Robin? Trey? It's Noah Cason and Chief Peterson. Open the door. I know you're there."

He stared through the window and spotted Robin approaching them. She unlocked the door. "We're closed."

Her face was bruised and her lip bloody. Noah pushed open the door she tried to keep closed. "What happened to your face?"

She touched her lip but was uncooperative. "Nothing. I slipped in the back. That's all."

"Really? Because it looks like someone beat you up. Who did this? Your husband? Ray Steele?"

She looked at him when he said Ray's name, and he knew he'd hit pay dirt.

"Is he here now?" He shoved past her and hurried into the kitchen. "Where is he, Robin? I know he's been here. I know you've been helping him."

She and Peterson followed him into the back.

"I don't know what you're talking about," she stated again. "No one is here."

Noah rushed at her. "He has Melinda and Ramey. I want to know where he is, Robin, and I want to know now."

She stared up at him, her face stricken. "I—I have no idea what you're talking about."

"I know you're involved in this," Noah told her. "You and your husband. The night Melinda and I came by, he made a phone call to Ray Steele to let him know we were here. He shot into your bakery. The two of you warned him. I want to know why, and I want to know where he's taken Melinda."

She clasped her hands together, but he could see she was frightened. He didn't know if it was because of him, or if she was too frightened to speak because she was afraid of Ray. He knelt beside her. "You were her friend, Robin. You were Melinda's friend. But you lured her to that restaurant so your friend Ray Steele could plant that bomb, and you told him how to get his hands on her son, too, didn't you?"

She glanced at him and gasped, but remained silent.

"Who else knew Susan was the only other person

who could pick up Ramey besides Melinda? You knew and you told him, didn't you? Did you know she's dead? Murdered right in front of her son."

She sobbed but didn't open her mouth to speak.

"You may as well tell us the truth, Robin," Peterson stated. "We're going to find out one way or another, and you don't want to add double murder to your charges."

"Double murder?"

"He used Ramey to lure Melinda to him. He has her, and we need to find her before he hurts either her or Ramey. It's already murder and kidnapping. Don't make it any worse."

She glanced at them both like she wanted to say something, then shook her head. "I can't. I have a family, too."

"We'll protect them," Peterson said.

"No, you can't. You can't protect us."

"Tell them the truth, Robin."

Noah jumped to his feet and drew his gun at the same time as Peterson. Trey Danbar stepped from the back.

He looked defeated and forlorn and repeated his instructions to his wife. "Tell them the truth."

Peterson rushed to him and patted him down for weapons, then led him over to his wife and forced him to sit beside her.

"Tell me what happened."

Trey did the talking. "He showed up here in town six weeks ago. He came looking for me."

"Why? How do you know him?"

"I don't, but I did some work for another guy. Apparently, Ray met him in prison and told him about me."

"What kind of work?" Noah demanded.

He lowered his eyes. "He hired me to launder money through my bank. He offered me a lot of money, and at the time we were in financial need. The bakery wasn't earning its potential and our son, Caleb, had to have surgery. I was in over my head, and we were going to lose the house. This guy approached me and offered me the opportunity to make big bucks. I took it and laundered the money. But even after I had caught up on all the bills and things were looking up, I couldn't get out. He kept wanting more and more, and I knew that soon I was going to be caught for what I was doing."

"I still haven't heard how you got involved with Ray."

"This guy I was laundering money for got arrested for dealing drugs. He went to prison. I thought I was free and clear. Then six weeks ago Ray showed up. He said he'd met Cooper in prison and learned all about me. He said I owed Cooper, and helping him was my way of paying Cooper back."

"So you agreed?"

"No. I flat-out refused. I was out. I told Ray to get lost."

"But he didn't?"

"No, he didn't. I came home from work one day, and he had Robin and Caleb tied up. He said he would kill them if I didn't tell him everything we knew about Melinda. We helped him only because he threatened our family."

Robin started to cry. "It's true. I lured her to that lunch so he could plant the bomb. He kept telling me I had to get her out of the office, but she kept refusing to meet with me. I panicked and just kept insisting." She put her hands on her face and sobbed quietly. "I didn't want any of this."

Noah knelt beside her. "I understand why this happened. He threatened your family. Now I need you to be strong. I need you to tell me where he's taken Melinda."

"We have a boat," Trey said. "It's docked down at the marina. He took the keys."

Peterson pulled out a small notebook. "Does this boat have GPS? I need the coordinates."

"I'll get them," Trey said, standing.

Peterson followed him into the office while Noah waited with Robin. He felt sorry for her, but he understood she was looking out for her family. Now she and her husband would be in jail, and her child would be left parentless. Ray had managed to destroy another family.

Peterson handcuffed them both to their respective chairs. "You're both under arrest for multiple accounts of attempted murder and conspiracy to kidnapping. You have the right to remain silent. Anything you say and do can be used against you in a court of law. You have the right to an attorney, and if you cannot afford an attorney, one will be appointed to you. Do you both understand these rights I've explained to you?"

"I do," Trey stated.

"So do I," Robin said.

"Good. I'll have an officer swing by and pick you up." He motioned toward Noah. "Let's go."

Noah knew leaving them here until another officer arrived wasn't proper police protocol even in a small town, but he was glad Peterson wasn't going to try to make him wait until someone else arrived.

"Isn't Melinda afraid of the water?" he asked as they hurried to the car. "Would she go to a marina?"

Noah knew the truth. "To save her son, she would do whatever she had to do."

And he would do whatever it took to bring them both home safely, even if he could never have a life with them.

NINE

Melinda parked the car at the marina and got out. She walked to the back and opened the trunk. She knew Noah kept weapons back here, and she dug through a bag until she found a handgun. She wasn't going to face Ray Steele without protection.

She hid the gun in her pocket then walked down the wooden pier, her heart pounding in time with her racing feet. Ray hadn't told her which boat, but she knew he would make it easy for her to find him. He wasn't hiding any longer.

She slowed as she spotted a familiar figure on a boat at the end of the pier. She recognized the way he moved and his manner. She sucked in a breath. Noah had assured her Sean was dead, but this man, even from this distance, could be him. She didn't miss the name of the boat he was on, either. *Robin's Nest*. This boat belonged to Trey and Robin Danbar. How had Ray gotten his hands on it? Had Noah been right that they were involved in this somehow? Or had Ray killed them as he'd killed Susan Campbell and taken their boat keys?

As she moved closer, the light hit his face, and she knew for certain. It wasn't Sean, but someone who looked an awful lot like him. Ray.

"I'm not sure we ever met," he said sarcastically as she approached. "Allow me to introduce myself. Ray Steele at your service."

She didn't flinch at his mocking tone. He could say and do whatever he wanted to her. All she cared about was Ramey. "Where's my son?"

"Down below." He moved out of her way and indicated for her to step onboard. "Care to see for yourself?"

Her knees nearly gave out, and she felt woozy as she glanced at the water between the pier and boat. It called to her like a lure, beckoning her to fall into its depths and be lost forever. On any other day, she might have run screaming from this sight, but she planted her feet. She couldn't run. She had to summon up the courage to step onto that boat without falling into hysteria. Ramey was depending on her.

She took a deep breath then stepped over the edge. She was shaking with fear, but determined not to let it stop her. She was no dummy. Ray couldn't be trusted. A part of her wished she'd told Noah where she was going and what she was doing, but she pushed those thoughts aside. She couldn't put her trust in another man, even Noah. Ramey had only her to protect him. She had no choice but to do everything Ray commanded.

He stopped her and patted her down, finding the gun she'd taken from Noah's trunk.

"Nice try," he sneered, tossing the weapon over the side into the water. He also took her cell phone and tossed it in, too.

Her heart dropped as she heard the splash. That gun had been their only means of escaping from Ray. Now they were truly at his mercy.

She walked toward the cabin as he untied the boat and started the engine. Her heart stopped at the way it rocked in the water, and panic threatened to overtake her. She held on to the cabin walls as she pushed open the door and saw her son, her baby, tied up and gagged.

"Ramey!" She ran to him and pulled him into a hug.

"Mommy!" His mouth was gagged and his voice came out only as a grunt, but she knew he'd called her name, and she could see the relief in his face.

She quickly unbound him, and he threw himself against her.

"I'm scared, Mommy."

"I know, baby. Everything is going to be okay. I'm here now. I'll take care of this."

But as she stared out the window and saw the land disappear in the distance and fog begin to roll in, she gulped and wondered if she would ever see land again.

Peterson drove him to the marina. It was nearly abandoned this time of night, but Noah spotted his rental parked. "There's my car."

Peterson pulled up next to it, and Noah hopped out. He scanned the horizon, grabbing a pair of binoculars Peterson had on the seat. He spotted a boat pulling away in the distance.

He handed the binoculars to Peterson and tried the door of his car. Melinda had left it unlocked, with the keys inside. He popped the trunk and grabbed his gear. He had a go bag complete with weapons, ammunition, night vision goggles and other assorted things he might need on a mission. "I'm going after them," he said, hurrying up the pier. Peterson ran behind him as he found a small boat and hopped aboard.

Peterson followed him. "What do you have planned?"

"Whatever it takes." Melinda may not trust him and would probably never want to be with him, but he wasn't going to just let Ray Steele get away with murder. She and Ramey deserved a good life away from the chaos and evil that this world kept throwing at them, and Noah was determined to give them that life, even if he couldn't be a part of it. It was the least he could do for them. He quickly hotwired the boat while Peterson untied it from the dock.

"I'll contact the Harbor Police," he said as he hopped back aboard and took out his cell phone.

Noah started the boat and took off after her. He had to keep an eye out for the boat. Fog had rolled in, making keeping up with the boat more difficult. He had to stay close enough to keep up with them without alerting Ray that he was being followed.

All his instincts were on alert. He wasn't leaving without Melinda and Ramey.

Lord, guide my way and keep them safe.

He was well trained and had performed several hostage rescues during his time with the SEALs, but he had several things going against him. He was emotionally involved in this rescue, and that could cloud his judgment, but it also made him more determined to bring them both home safely. Secondly, he was used to working as a team. He was alone on this mission except for Peterson. He'd proven himself trustworthy, but Noah had no idea what he was capable of. No, he was on his own for this mission.

Except that he wasn't. He'd never truly been alone. He had God on his side. Noah felt His presence beside him, keeping him calm in the face of tragedy and guiding his thoughts. Like Melinda, he'd never been one to trust others, but he'd never had something as important to him before as Melinda and Ramey. His skills alone might not be enough to save them, but God could. He had to trust in that. Noah still had no answers about why God would allow evil and chaos to reign, but that didn't matter now. God had always been with him and given Noah the strength and ability to overcome the evil he encountered. He prayed this time would be no different.

"The Harbor Guard is on their way," Peterson stated as he put away his phone. He glanced at the ship in the distance. It had stopped. "What's the plan?"

Noah brought the boat to a halt, then unzipped his go bag and pulled out his air tank. "I'm going to swim over and board that boat. Melinda and Ramey might already be in danger."

He stripped off his jacket, overshirt and his socks and shoes. His go bag also contained guns, one of which he tucked into his waistband.

He jumped into the water and swam toward the boat,

his strokes long and sure. The water was cold, but he'd trained in colder. This was the moment he'd spent his life training for. He quickly closed the distance between them, and the closer he got to the ship, the less he heard—only the lap of the water. He started to hear voices floating over the air, and the more he heard, the faster his arms and legs pushed him.

God, please guide my path. Keep them safe. Keep them safe.

This moment was the fulfillment of his life's purpose. He was alone in the water, fighting for his life, but he'd been preparing for this moment for so long. His childhood had taught him to stand up against evil, and the SEALs had given him the skills to do so. Even his time with SOA had given him the isolation and time he needed to know that he didn't want to spend his life alone. He wanted a family and all the things that came with it. He wanted Melinda, and he wanted to teach and guide Ramey to be a man his mother could be proud of. He may never get the opportunity because even if he saved her, Melinda might never forgive him, but he would fight for them with his last breath if necessary.

The cabin door burst open, and Ray entered. He saw Ramey untied and curled into her arms and growled, then grabbed the boy and pulled him up the steps.

Melinda screamed and ran after him. "Don't, Ray! Please don't hurt him! He has nothing to do with this."

Ray stopped and spun around to face her. "He shouldn't even be here, Melinda. You shouldn't be here, either. You took my brother from me. Now I'm taking your son."

"No! Ray, please, I didn't mean to kill him. I was just trying to survive. I didn't mean it. It was an accident."

Ray ignored her pleas and grabbed a roll of duct tape. He taped up the boy's hands and feet. Tears rolled down Ramey's face as he covered his mouth. She could see how his arms longed to reach out to her, and her own heart fell. Sobs racked her body. She tried to lunge at Ray and grab Ramey, but he easily held her off.

"You think you can hurt my family?" Ray demanded of Melinda. "No one messes with the Steeles without paying the price." He lifted Ramey, then tossed him into the water. Melinda screamed and ran for the edge, but Ray grabbed her, pulling her back.

"No!" she cried, hitting her knees. She couldn't hear Ramey's cries, and that terrified her even more.

Ray shoved her back away from the edge. She fell to her knees, her sobs coming harder than she could stop. Ray had taken everything from her. She fell to the floor and cried. He jeered at her, laughing at her pain. This had been his plan all along. To take everything from her and laugh at her suffering.

She looked up at him. "Why would you do that? He was an innocent child. He never did anything to you!"

Ray knelt beside her. "He was an abomination. My brother never wanted him here, so it's better that he's gone."

She shivered at the coldness in his face. She'd seen that same apathy in Sean's eyes. He hadn't wanted a child, but Ramey had been a gift, a blessing to her, the one thing that pushed her to keep going when life seemed so intolerable. Now, he was gone. It was unfair and cruel and wrong and nothing would ever be right in her world again. "What are you going to do with me?"

"I'm going to kill you eventually. But first I'll let you sit for a while with the knowledge that everything you've built is gone. You took my brother from me. Now I've taken everything from you, and soon I'll take your life, too. First, I'll make you suffer even more."

He tied her to the bar and walked back into the cabin of the boat.

Melinda leaned against the edge and wept. What more could she suffer? Her world was gone. Ray had taken everything from her. She had no words to form to ask why God would allow such a thing to happen. She'd just watched her child die. What worse thing could Ray do to her?

She slipped into a state where she didn't care. Shock had surely set in because all she felt was emptiness inside. She was going to die. She'd lost everything, including the will to live. Then she remembered Noah. She'd lost him, too. She was going to die with him believing she blamed him. She didn't. She never had. He'd just been a convenient sounding board for her grief. She grimaced at the terrible accusations she'd hurled at him. Her heart broke as she realized her last words to him would be words of condemnation and anger. She hadn't meant it. She hadn't meant any of it.

God had sent her a warrior to fight for her, and she'd pushed him away.

* * *

Noah held on to Ramey as the noise from the boat grew quieter. The boy was doing great at keeping quiet so Ray wouldn't hear them as they swam away. Noah hated leaving Melinda on that boat, but knew she would want him to save Ramey first.

He whistled, and Peterson turned on a flashlight and shone it into the water. Noah lifted Ramey from the water, and Peterson pulled him over the edge. Noah climbed aboard, too. He pulled out his knife and cut the duct tape around his feet and hands and pulled it from his mouth.

"Are you hurt?" he asked Ramey.

The boy shook his head, but his eyes were wide with fear. "I want my mommy," he whispered.

Noah patted his shoulder. "I'm going back for her right now." There was no way he was going to leave her with a madman who'd already proven that killing a child wasn't outside his scope of evil. "While I do, you need to stay here with Chief Peterson and be very quiet. Can you do that for me?"

Ramey glanced up at Peterson then back to Noah. He nodded. "I can be quiet." Noah doubted he was in any mood to run and jump. He was too frightened for that.

He stood, and Peterson leaned in to speak so the boy couldn't hear. "Was she there? Did you see her?"

"Yes, he has her tied up on the bow. Told her he wants to give her time to realize everything he's taken from her."

"So she doesn't know you have Ramey?"

"No, I couldn't get close enough to tell her without Ray seeing me." It had broken his heart to hear her cries and not be able to reassure her, but if he could help it, she would soon be reunited with her son. "Hopefully, I can get back to her before Ray decides she's had enough."

"Harbor Patrol has a boat on the way. I told them to come in with their lights off when they reached these coordinates."

"Hold them off until I can get Melinda out safely."

"How will I know when that is?"

"If I'm not back with her in ten minutes, send help."

He winked at Ramey to assure him everything was fine, then jumped from the boat back into the water and started swimming in the direction of the boat that held Melinda.

His heart beat a steady thump in the water. He stopped as the boat came into view. Melinda was still on the bow alone. Ray was nowhere in sight. That was good news. He swam the rest of the way under water so he wouldn't be detected by Ray if he happened to step out of the cabin.

He reached the side of the boat and found a place he could climb aboard. The moment his feet hit the floor, he pulled his gun. He hurried toward the front and saw her, duct-taped to a railing, slumped over and sobbing.

He rushed to her and put away his gun, taking out his knife instead. "Melinda, it's me."

She glanced up at him through red eyes and wet hair.

"It's me, Noah. Are you okay?" He used his knife to slice through the tape and free her hands.

"He killed Ramey," she cried as she fell into his arms.

"Ramey's fine. I was in the water when he threw him overboard. He's on a boat behind the rocks."

She stared into his face and saw doubt and suspicion, but also a ray of hope. "Ramey's alive?"

"Yes. I promised you I would keep him safe." He touched her face as all the love he felt for her surfaced. "I love you, Melinda. I know I don't deserve you, and you can never trust your heart to someone like me, but I do love you." He watched her face for some sign that she felt the same way he did, but her face morphed and her eyes widened. He heard the movement behind him, but it was too late to do anything about it.

He spun around just as Ray swung a crowbar and hit him in the head. Melinda screamed as Noah hit the deck and pain radiated through him. He resisted the urge to lose consciousness. If he did, they were both dead. Instead, he tried to push himself up, but Ray swung at him again.

Darkness fell over him, and the last things he heard were the gentle lap of the lake and the sobs from the woman he loved.

The elation she'd felt only a moment before when Noah had told her Ramey was safe dissipated as she saw Noah collapse on the deck.

Ray threw down the crowbar and heaved until he had Noah over his shoulders.

Her heart stopped when she heard the splash of his body hitting the water. She ran to the edge and saw him floating facedown. He was unconscious and wouldn't last long without air.

Ray turned to her, fire in his eyes. "Now you," he sneered.

But she had a newfound reason to fight. Her son was alive, and it was because of Noah. And he'd said he loved her. He'd come for her despite how she'd pushed him away, and he'd rescued Ramey. How could she have ever doubted him? She had to do whatever she could to protect the man she loved.

She looked at Ray, who was laughing over killing someone else she loved. His cruelty sparked a newfound fire inside Melinda. She wasn't going to allow another man to try to take her family from her without a fight. She swooped up the crowbar he'd just used to attack Noah and swung it at him, hitting him over the head while his back was turned. Ray screamed then hit his knees. She reared back again and brought it down on his head. He hit the floor and sprawled out, unconscious.

She tossed the crowbar and ran to the edge. Noah wasn't moving. He was still facedown in the water, and the waves were taking him farther away.

God, please don't take him now! Not before I get the chance to tell him how sorry I am and how much I love him!

She searched for something to grab him with and pull him back to the boat. She found a net and tried to reach him, but it was too far.

Finally, she knew the truth. She had no choice but to go in after him.

Fear gripped her at the thought of entering the water. She wasn't sure she was going to be able to do it, but Noah's life depended on her reaching him in time, and she wasn't giving up on him again. She thought about Peter, the apostle of Jesus, stepping out onto the water in faith. He'd believed so strongly that Jesus was there with him that he'd walked on the water.

She wasn't asking for nearly as much. All she wanted was to reach Noah in time and have faith enough to know that God would protect her while she did so. If he'd been there with Peter, he was surely there for her, too.

She held on to that faith and gathered up her courage as she slipped into the water. Melinda held on to the boat as panic threatened to paralyze her. She couldn't allow it to get the better of her. She had to reach him. She pushed off the boat and slowly, cautiously, moved toward Noah.

She pushed through the fear in the knowledge that God was with her. Despite all she'd been through, He'd been with her, fighting for her, giving her the strength to survive Sean's attack on her life, the strength to go through law school and raise a child on her own. He'd even sent her a warrior when she'd needed one. He had never abandoned her, and He never would.

She reached Noah and raised his head from the water. He was bleeding and unconscious. She had to get him back to the boat. She pulled him back, but even with the water sustaining his weight, it wasn't easy. But before she reached the boat, she heard the engine start up and saw Ray speed away.

Her heart dropped. What would they do now? Noah had mentioned a boat hidden behind the rocks. But she wasn't sure she had the strength to pull him that far.

Suddenly, he roused and opened his eyes. When he realized where he was and what was happening, he quickly came back to life.

"What happened?"

"Ray attacked you. He threw you overboard. Now he's gone."

He touched her face. "You came after me? In the water?"

She nodded.

"How did you do that?"

"I couldn't let you die. I love you. I would do anything to save you."

He stared at her. "Did you say you love me?"

"I did. I do. I'm sorry, Noah. I'm sorry for what I said to you. I do trust you. I trust you with my life and with Ramey's."

"But I—I let you down."

"No, you didn't. You're the only one who's been there for me." She reached out and stroked his face, basking in the feel of his strength and endurance. "There's no one in this world I trust more than you, Noah Cason. I love you."

He kissed her, and his arms went around her.

Suddenly, she was fine, all her fear vanished. She was safe in the water, safe in his arms, and she wasn't afraid.

"Melinda, will you do something for me? Will you marry me?"

She looked at him, so full of love and hope after what they'd just been through. "You have a head wound. I think you're delirious."

"I'm not delirious. I'm in love. With you. Melinda Steele, will you be my wife?"

She laughed at the silliness of it all, but she'd never known a love like Noah's. If it was her lot to die in this water, at least she would die happy in his arms. "Yes, I will marry you, Noah. I love you."

He kissed her long and hard, and she basked in his embrace as they treaded water together.

Suddenly, a noise grabbed her. She heard the *thump thump* and saw a light hit the water, sweeping over the area. They both looked up at a helicopter hovering over them.

"Who is that?"

"Harbor Patrol. They were waiting behind the island until I rescued you. They would have activated when Ray tried to motor away." He waved up to them.

A boat sped up beside them, and life preservers were thrown off. Noah grabbed one and wrapped it around her, then swam to the boat. She saw Chief Peterson leaning over the side, reaching down for her.

"I've got you," he said as he grabbed her arm and lifted her over the side. She spotted Ramey as her feet touched the floor. He was huddled in the front by the steering wheel, a life preserver wrapped around him and his arms and knees huddled together.

She called his name, and he looked up. His face lit up and he jumped to his feet and ran to her. She held him tightly, so thankful he was safe.

"Are you okay?" she asked him.

"I was so scared, Mommy, but Noah saved me."

She turned and saw Noah climbing over the side of the boat. Blood was gushing from the wound on his head, and he was wet from head to toe, but he looked strong and virile. He'd saved them both.

She went to him and slid into his embrace, and he closed his arms around her. Ramey ran to them, pushing himself between them and into their hug. They both laughed, and Noah looked down and kissed her.

"I love you, Noah Cason," she told him.

She basked in the warmth of his arms, content in never leaving them.

Noah readied his weapon as Chief Peterson motioned for his team to move in on the bakery. He wasn't an official member of Peterson's team, but there was no way he was going to miss out on taking Ray Steele down.

The Robin's Nest had been found abandoned onshore an hour ago, and Noah figured Ray would return to a place he was familiar with. He proved correct when a shadowed figure entered the back door of the bakery. He stumbled through the room and went straight for the cash register, opening it and yanking out the cash.

Noah flipped on the light and Ray spun around, his eyes now looking down the barrel of Noah's gun.

Ray sneered at him. "You going to shoot me now? Go ahead and get it over with."

Part of him wanted to take the shot and rid the Earth of one more weed. This man had terrorized Melinda and Ramey all because his brother had failed at killing them.

"He's all yours," Noah said as Peterson and his team appeared and surrounded Ray. One of them stepped forward, grabbed his arms and cuffed his hands behind his back. "Ray Steele, you are under arrest for kidnapping, murder and attempted murder." Noah heard him issuing his Miranda rights as they led Ray Steele away and out of their lives.

"How is Melinda?" Peterson asked. "Still at the hospital?"

"Yes, but they're not keeping her. In fact, I'm supposed to be picking her up and taking her home right now, but I had to be here. I had to make sure this man was out of our lives for good."

Peterson clapped his shoulder. "He is, and he won't be getting out anytime soon. We have enough physical evidence from Dawn Littlefield and Susan Campbell's crime scenes to convict him. And of course, we have Melinda and Ramey's testimonies about the kidnappings."

"What about the Danbars?"

"He's facing money laundering charges, but I doubt we'll be able to pin anything on Robin. We'll have to let her go soon."

"I hope she has the good sense to stay away from Melinda."

"My guess is she'll grab her son and sneak quietly out of town to start over."

Noah said his farewells and left Peterson to finish booking Ray Steele. He didn't need to be there for that part. Just knowing that man was being locked up for good was enough for him.

He drove to the hospital, then stopped by the gift shop and picked up a bouquet of flowers for Melinda and a stuffed toy for Ramey. He took the elevator to the third floor and headed for her room at the end of the hall. As he entered, he saw her sitting on the sofa, Ramey curled up in her arms as she read a story to him.

She smiled when she saw him, and he walked over and leaned down to kiss her. Ramey grabbed the stuffed animal and pressed it to him, then prodded his mom to keep reading.

"Go ahead," Noah told her, taking the spot next to her on the sofa and wrapping his arms around them both. She leaned into him, and Ramey lay against her.

All was right in his world.

EPILOGUE

Melinda heard squeals of delight from outside the cabin. She recognized Ramey's voice and glanced out the window. Noah and Ramey were untying a Christmas tree from the top of his car. She pushed open the door and made room for them to enter.

They were still at the cabin. She'd made arrangements to rent it out through the holidays, or until her house could be rebuilt. And Noah, being the sweet man he was, decided the place needed a Christmas tree.

She had to admit she'd experienced a moment of fear when she'd watched Ramey hop into the car with Noah and disappear down the road, but she had faith in Noah, and that feeling of fear soon passed. She was learning to trust again, but it didn't come easily. Noah was patient with her, and understanding, willing to give her the time she needed to recover.

He carried the tree inside and placed it in an empty corner he'd cleaned out earlier. The smell of pine filled the house, and the scent was uplifting and familiar.

"You didn't happen to pick up any ornaments for

it, did you?" she asked. "You know all of ours got lost in the fire."

He smiled and turned to her, and Ramey laughed like they both had a big secret. "Actually, I thought we might go into town together and get some. They're having the official lighting of the Christmas tree downtown. We can grab some ice cream and shop for decorations. How does that sound?"

"It sounds great!" Ramey exclaimed. "I want ice cream."

She laughed. "Now you've left me no choice. He won't stop talking about ice cream until he gets some."

Noah put his arm around her waist and kissed her. "Then let's go get some."

By the time they reached downtown, the tree and lights had already been lit, and the downtown center was aglow with Christmas lights and people swirling around. This really was a beautiful place, and the town went all out at Christmas.

As Ramey and Noah chomped down on ice cream cones, Melinda opted for hot chocolate. The night was colder than she could remember it being in a long time, and the forecast was even teasing about snow, something that rarely ever happened in Alabama.

She spotted Chief Peterson approaching them and waved. "Hi, how are you?"

He looked pensive and tired. This entire episode had taken a toll on him. "I have news. I didn't know whether I should wait or not, so I'm just going to tell you. I sent Wayne's GPS records to a tech guy in the Birmingham PD, and he was able to triangulate where

Wayne was the night before Nikki disappeared. We coordinated a search party." He glanced at Noah. "We recovered her body an hour ago."

She glanced at Noah and could see this news hit him hard. He'd been prepared for this, expected it even, but how did someone ever really prepare for news like this? She put her arm around him.

"Thank you for letting us know, Chief."

He looked at Noah. "I'm sorry for your loss. If it makes you feel better, I'm on my way to arrest Wayne for her murder."

"It does." Noah took a deep breath. "I wish I could be there to see his face, but I have other—" he pulled Melinda and Ramey tight against him "—more important plans tonight."

"Understood," Chief Peterson said. "Have a good night."

She glanced up at Noah to see how he was processing all of this. "Are you okay? It's big news."

"Yes, it is. Very big. But Wayne will get his due justice for what he did to her. Now at least we can have a funeral."

She smiled up at him. "That's true. Many people will be happy about that. She was loved here. Will you bury her here in town?"

He nodded. "This was her home. She belongs here." He glanced down at Melinda and Ramey. "And now so do I…if you'll have me."

He pulled a box from his pocket and opened it, then knelt on one knee. It was like a fairy-tale moment. The lights, the music playing in the square, even Ramey standing there with a big, silly grin on his face.

"I love you, Melinda. Ramey and I have been talking, and we were hoping we could all be a family. You made me a promise out there in the water. I hope you haven't changed your mind about it. Will you marry me?"

She glanced down at the two most important men in her life and realized how God had truly blessed her.

"I would love to marry you, Noah. I love you and I want to spend the rest of my life with you."

She walked out into the night, hand in hand with every Christmas wish she'd ever dreamed of.

* * * * *

*Don't miss the first book in the
Covert Operatives series by Virginia Vaughan:*

Cold Case Cover-Up

Available now from Love Inspired Suspense!

Find more great reads at www.LoveInspired.com

Dear Reader,

Does it ever seem to you that the bad people of the world get a pass and justice is never served? Sometimes it feels that way to me, and this is the very issue Noah is fighting with throughout the story. All he wants is justice for his sister, but it seems to elude him. He's disillusioned by all the evil and chaos he's seen and wondering how a good God can allow it.

But as Noah learns, we must have faith. We have a God who is always on His throne. He doesn't sleep. He's never absent. And He doesn't have to wonder whether or not someone is guilty of evil deeds. He doesn't need to collect evidence or proof. He knows. He sees into the hearts of men and gives justice to those who have been wronged. Sometimes, like Noah, we get to see justice done in our lifetimes, but we must never despair that God is the ultimate judge and His justice will always prevail.

Thank you for joining me for Noah and Melinda's story. I love hearing from my readers. You can connect with me on my website, virginiavaughanonline.com, or at Facebook.com/ginvaughanbooks.

Sincerely,
Virginia

Get 4 FREE REWARDS!

We'll send you 2 FREE Books
plus <u>2 FREE Mystery Gifts.</u>

Love Inspired® Suspense books feature Christian characters facing challenges to their faith... and lives.

FREE Value Over $20

Toby Potter watched the flames shoot toward the sky as he raced toward the building. "Robin!"

Sirens screamed closer. Toby had been on his way home when he'd spotted Robin's car in the parking lot of the lab. Ever since Robin had discovered his deception—orders to get close to her and figure out what was going on in the lab—she'd kept him at arm's length, her narrow-eyed stare hot enough to singe his eyebrows if he dare try to get too close.

Tonight, he'd planned to apologize profusely—again—and ask if there was anything he could do to earn her trust back. Only to pull into the parking lot, be greeted by the loud boom and watch flames shoot out of the window near the front door.

Heart pounding, Toby scanned the front door and rushed forward only to be forced back by the intense heat. Smoke billowed toward the dark night sky while the fire grew hotter and bigger. Mini explosions followed. Chemicals.

"Robin!"

Toby jumped into his truck and drove around to the back only to find it not much better, although it did seem to be more smoke than flames. Robin was in that building, and he was afraid he'd failed to protect her. Big-time.

Toby parked near the tree line in case more explosions were coming.

At the back door, he grasped the handle and pulled. Locked. Of course. Using both fists, he pounded on the glass-and-metal door. "Robin!"

Another explosion from inside rocked Toby back, but he was able to keep his feet under him. He figured the blast was on the other end of the building—where he knew Robin's station was. If she was anywhere near that station, there was no way she was still alive. "No, please no," he whispered. No one was around to hear him, but maybe God was listening.

Don't miss
Holiday Amnesia *by Lynette Eason,*
available December 2018 wherever
Love Inspired® Suspense books and ebooks are sold.

www.LoveInspired.com